pocket.watch

RYAN'S WORLD

RED TITAN AND THE RUNAWAY ROBOT

R

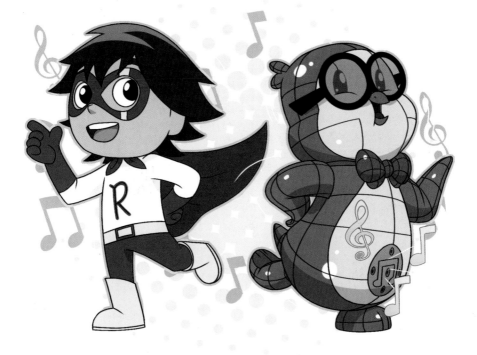

SIMON SPOTLIGHT
An imprint of Simon & Schuster Children's Publishing Division
1230 Avenue of the Americas, New York, New York 10020
This Simon Spotlight edition September 2021
Text by Arie Kaplan

For more information about special discounts for bulk purchases, please contact
Simon & Schuster Special Sales at 1-866-506-1949 or business@simonandschuster.com.
Manufactured in the United States of America 0322 LAK
4 6 8 10 9 7 5
ISBN 978-1-6659-0179-6 (hc)
ISBN 978-1-6659-0178-9 (pbk)
ISBN 978-1-6659-0180-2 (ebook)

pocket.watch RYAN'S WORLD

RED TITAN AND THE RUNAWAY ROBOT

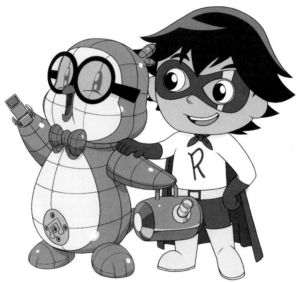

by **RYAN KAJI**
written by **ARIE KAPLAN**
illustrated by **PATRICK SPAZIANTE**

Ready-to-Read *GRAPHICS*

Simon Spotlight
New York London Toronto Sydney New Delhi

HOW TO READ THIS BOOK

Ryan is here to give you some tips on reading this book.

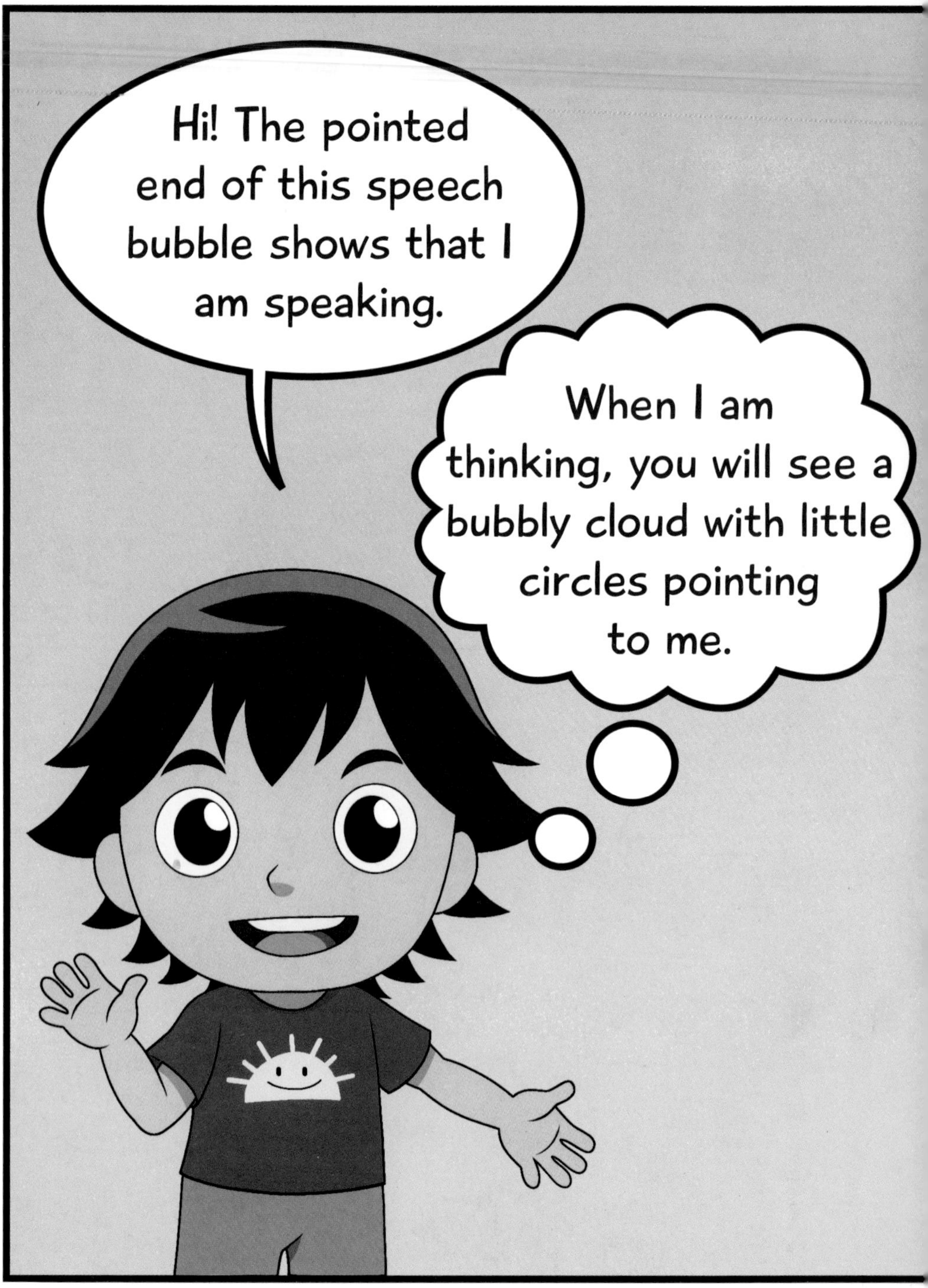
Hi! The pointed end of this speech bubble shows that I am speaking.
When I am thinking, you will see a bubbly cloud with little circles pointing to me.

It was a beautiful, sunny day. Ryan was flying a kite with his parents.

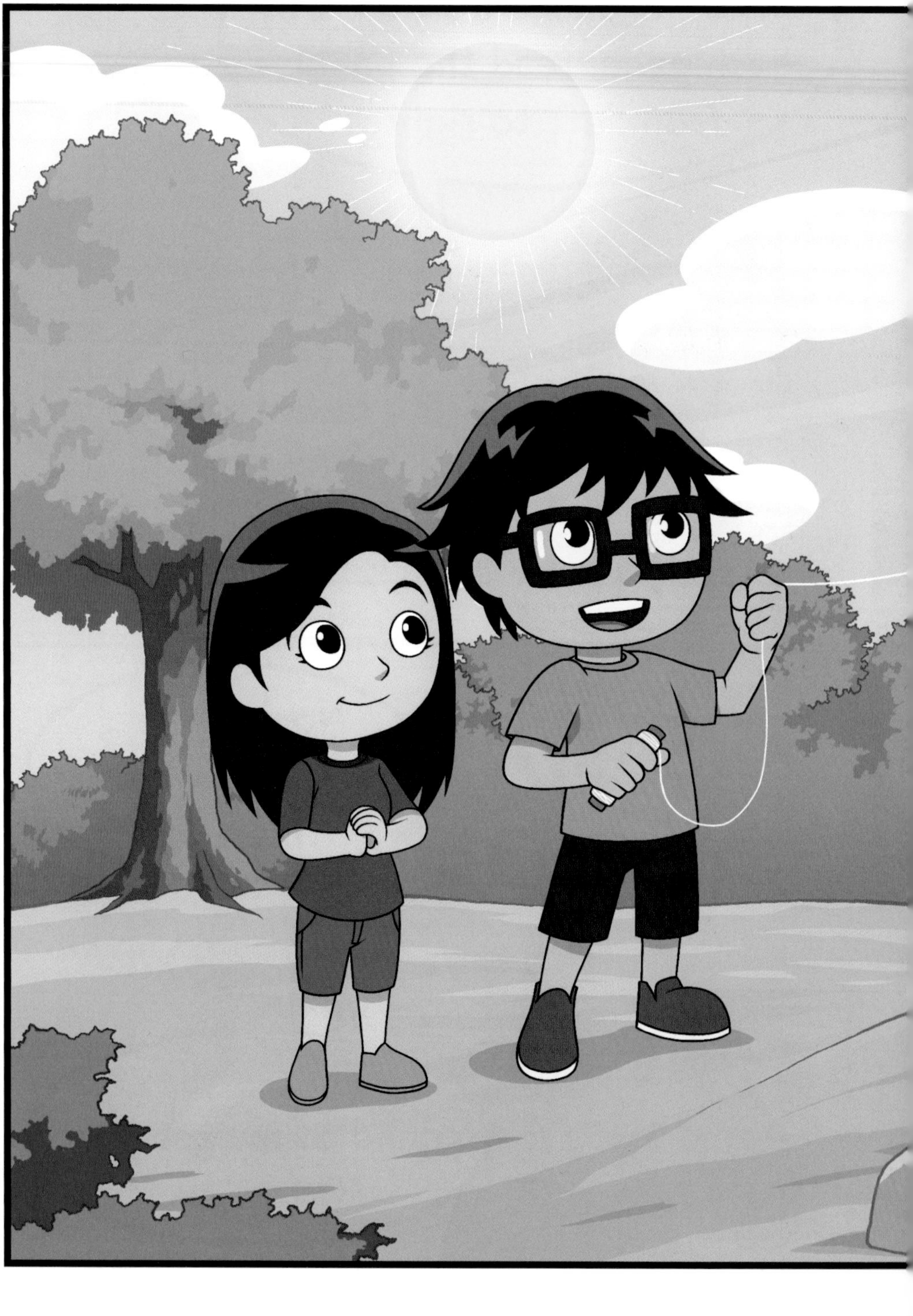

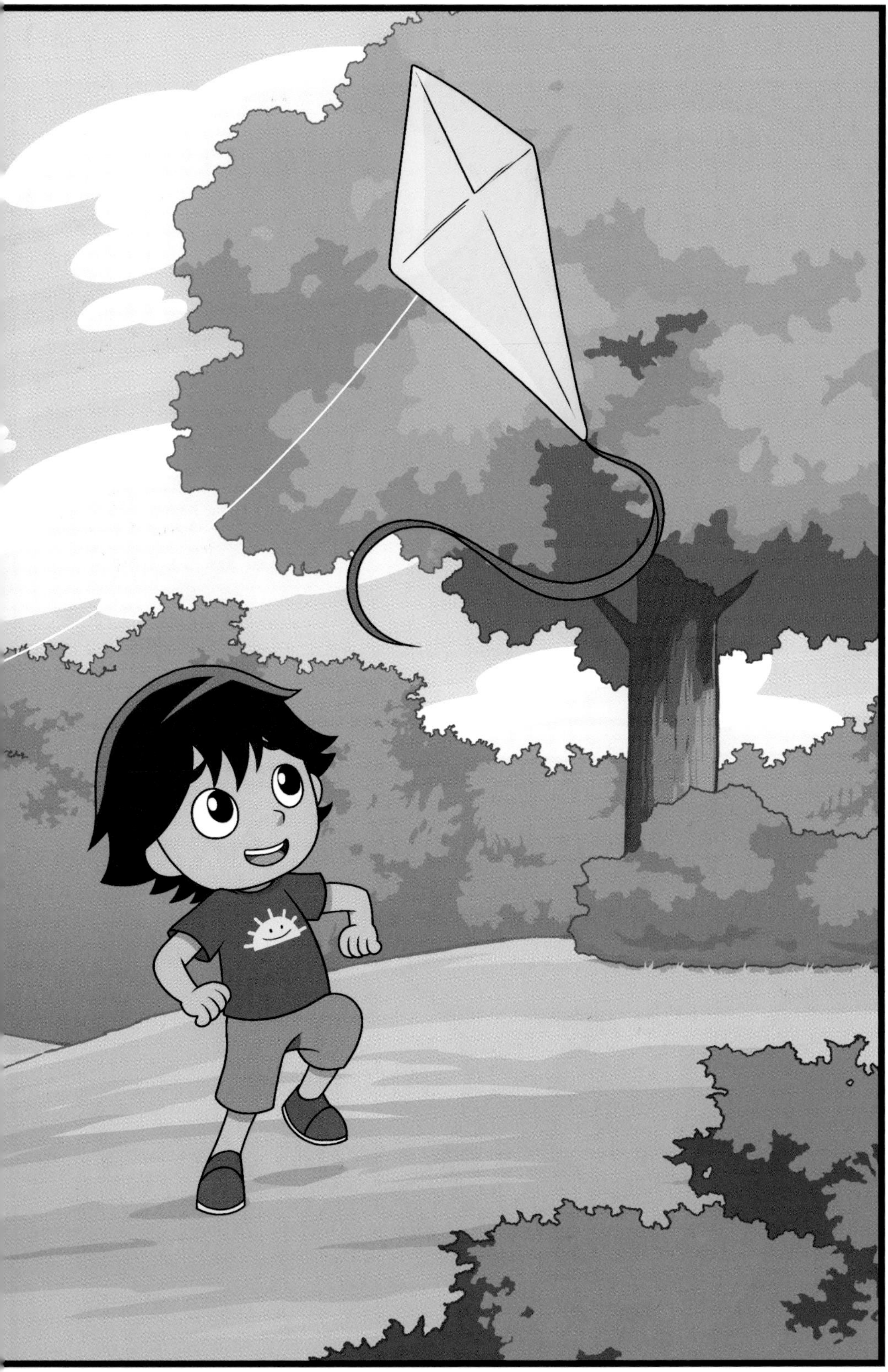

Just then...

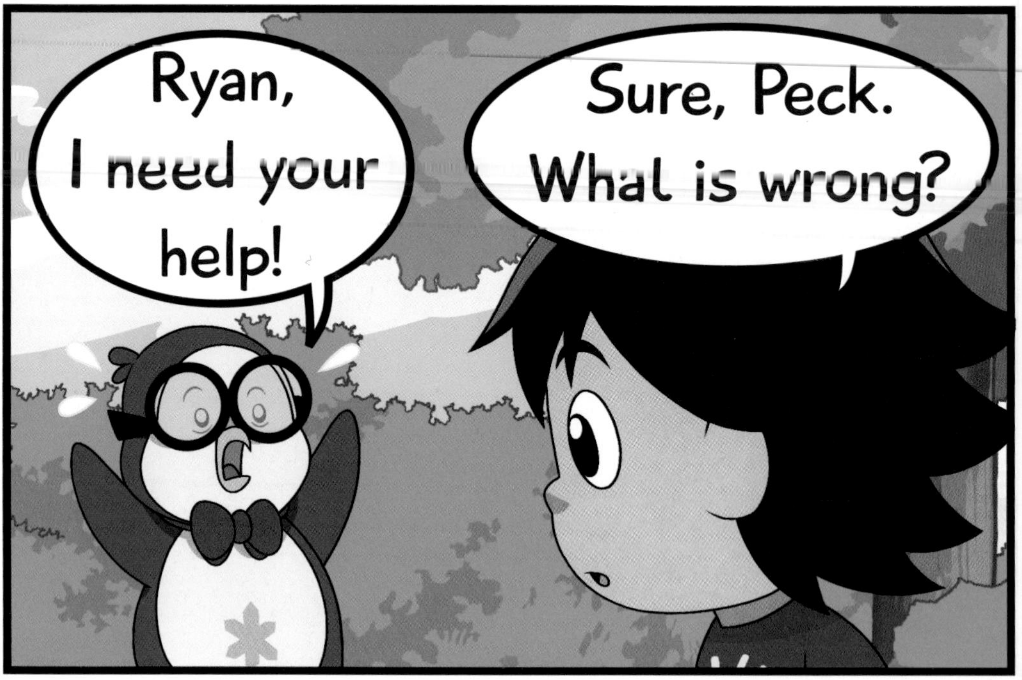
Ryan, I need your help!
Sure, Peck. What is wrong?

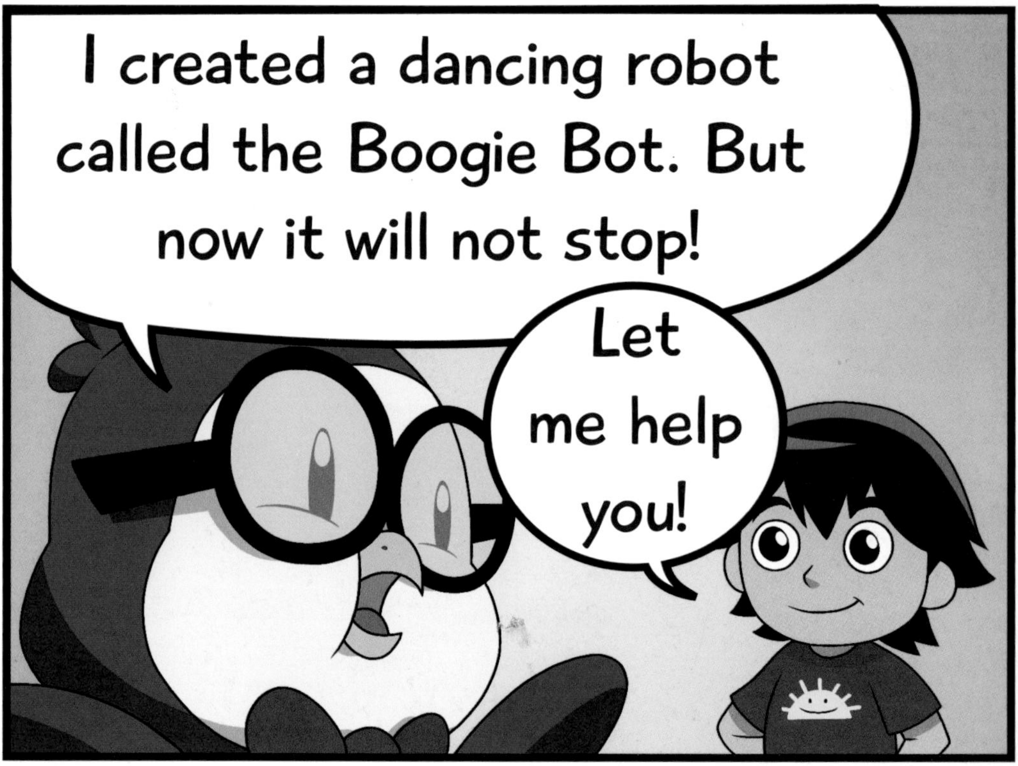
I created a dancing robot called the Boogie Bot. But now it will not stop!
Let me help you!

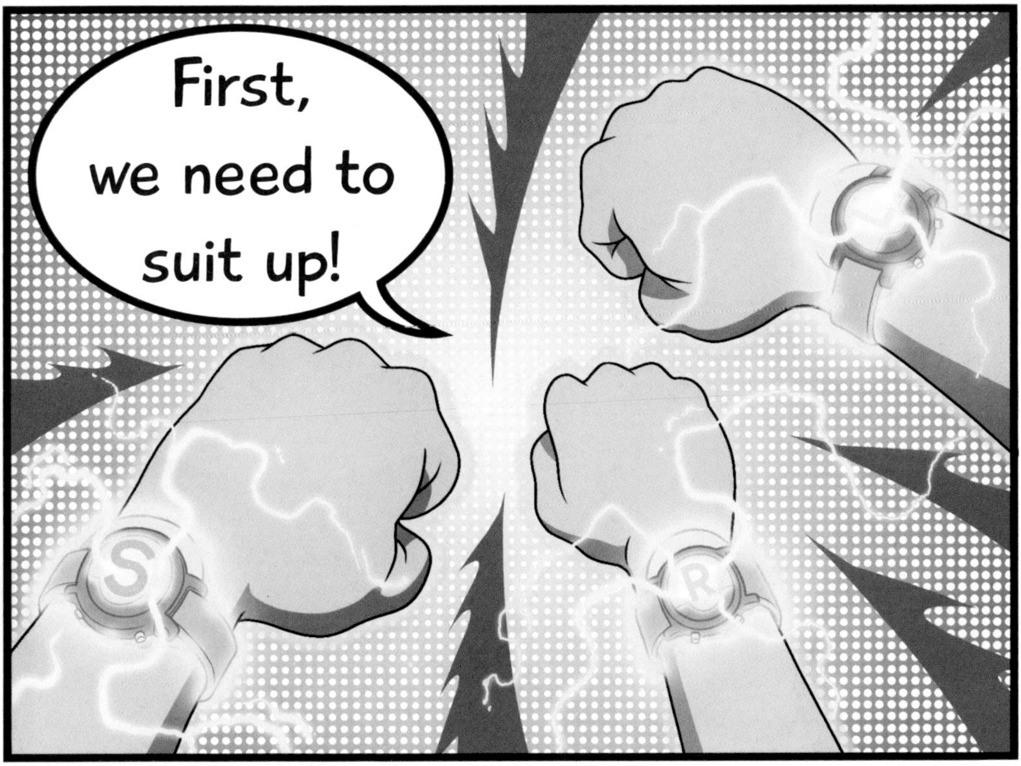
First, we need to suit up!

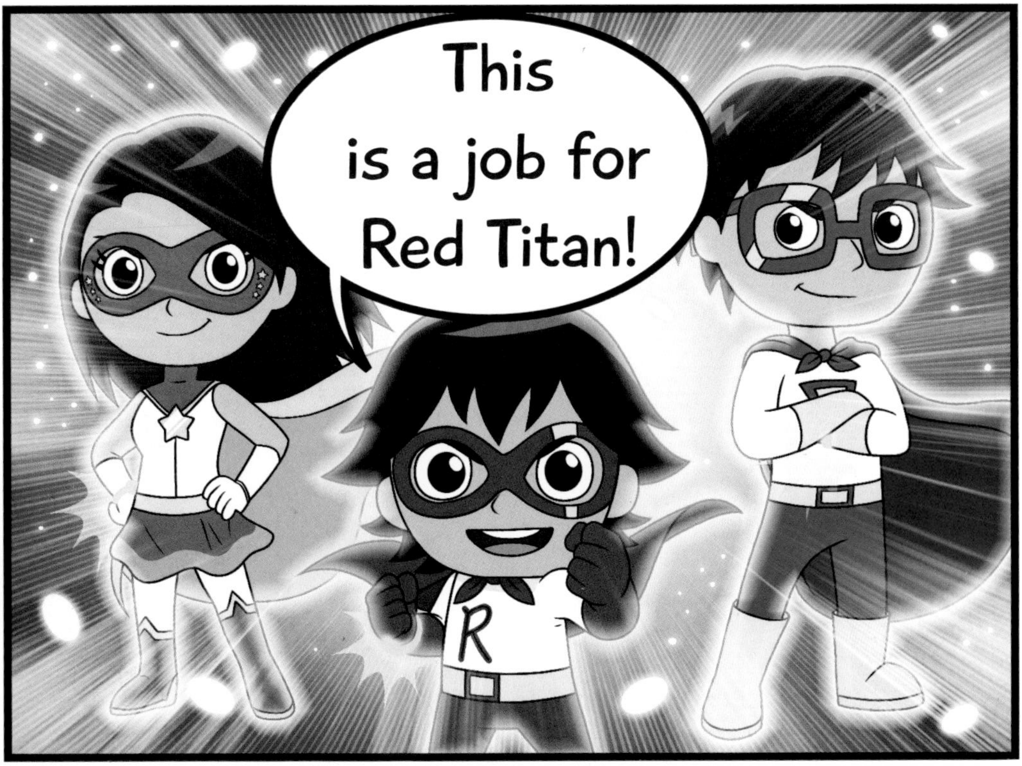
This is a job for Red Titan!

Moments later, at the lab...

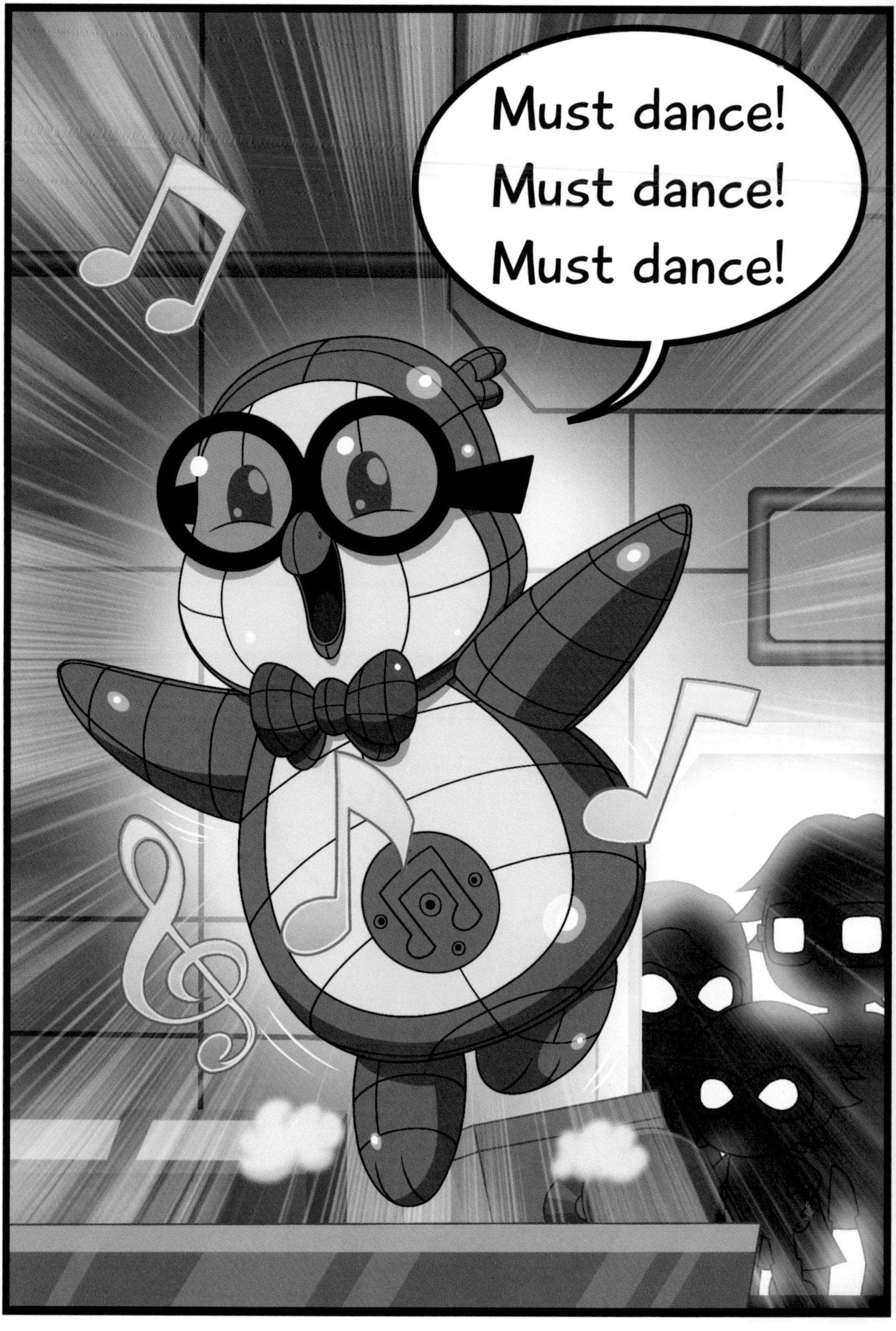
Must dance!
Must dance!
Must dance!

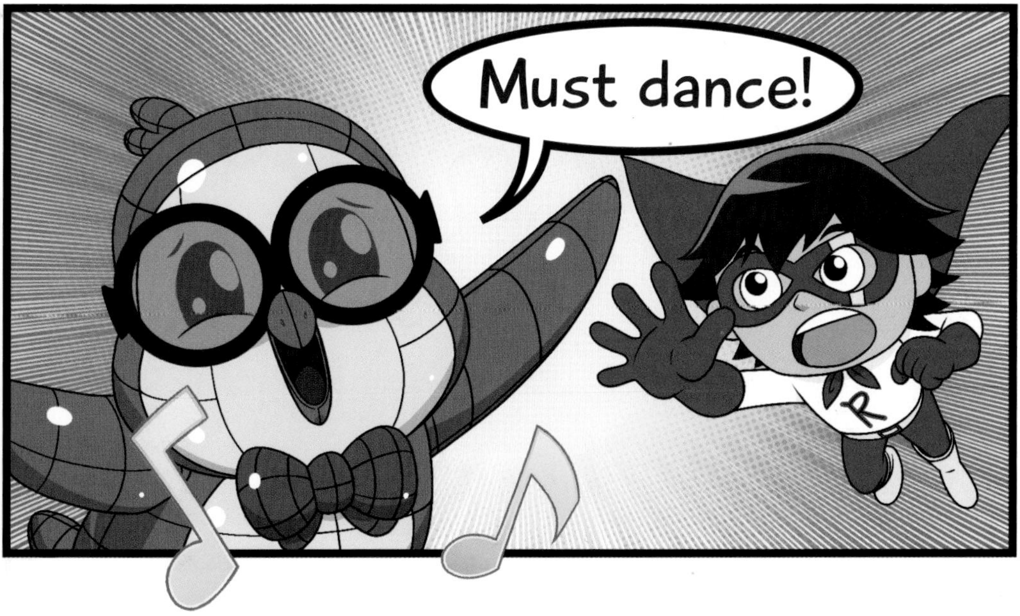
Must dance!

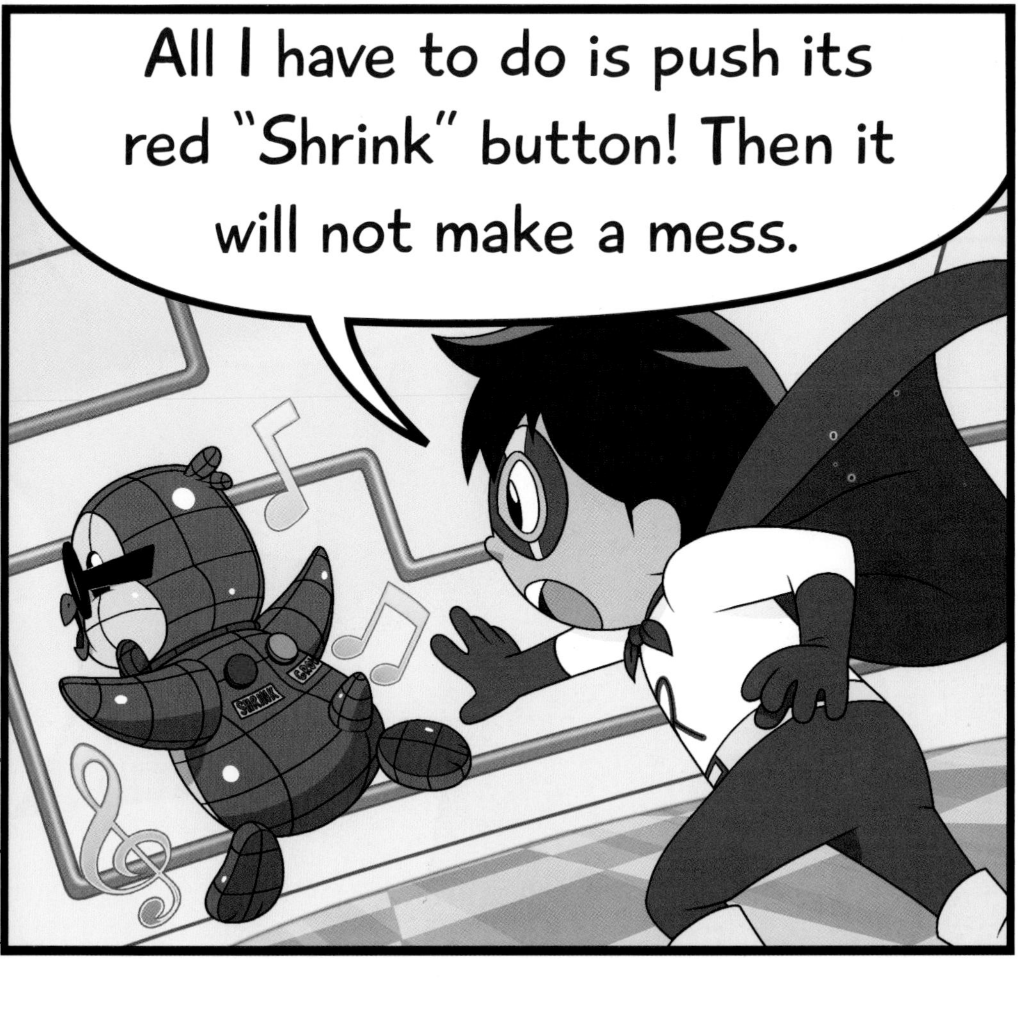
All I have to do is push its red "Shrink" button! Then it will not make a mess.
SHRINK

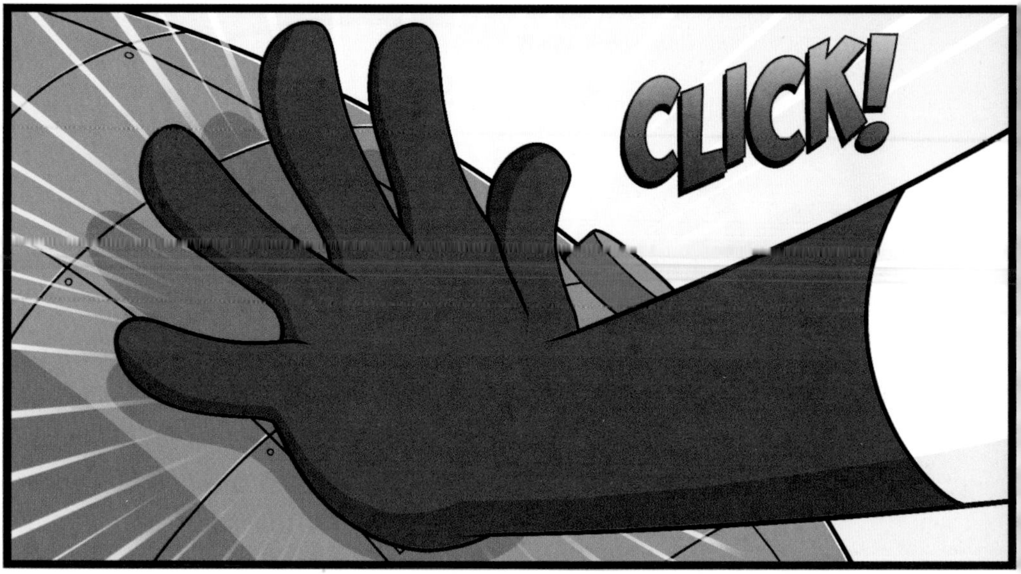
CLICK!

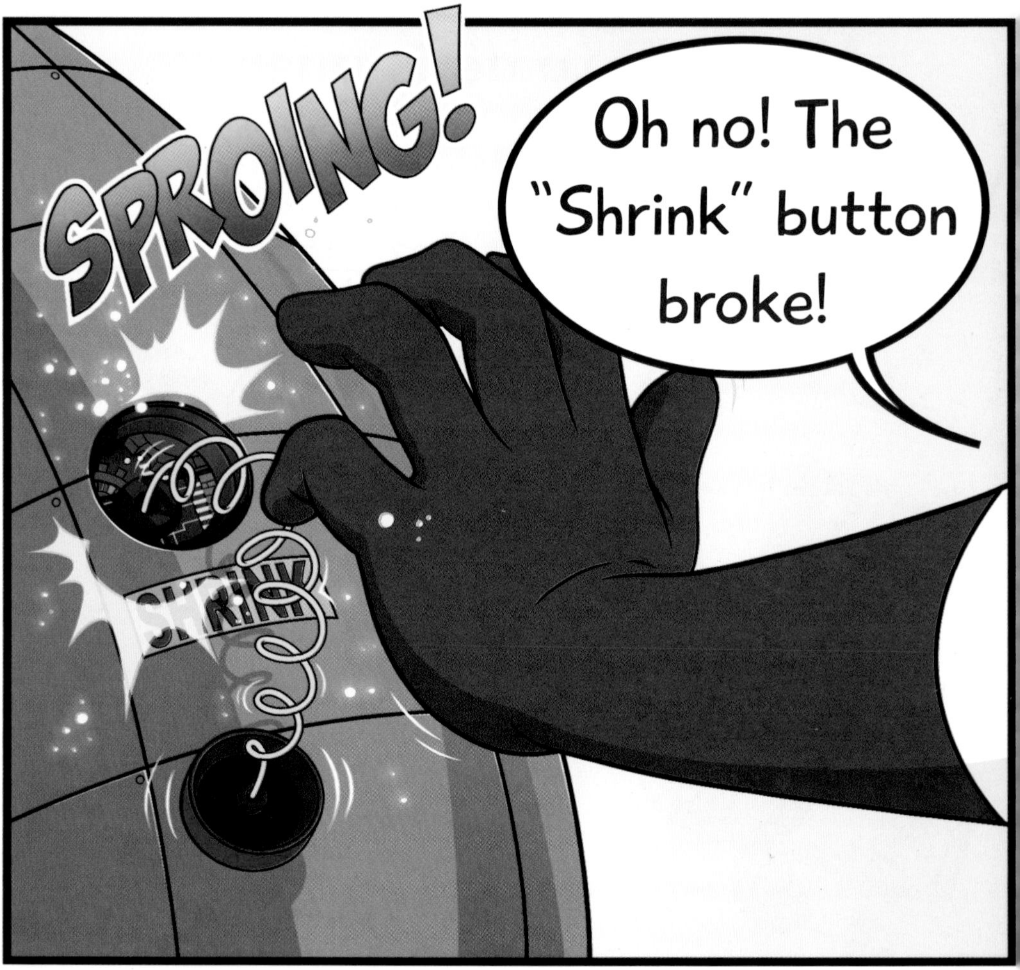
SPROING!
Oh no! The "Shrink" button broke!
SHRINK

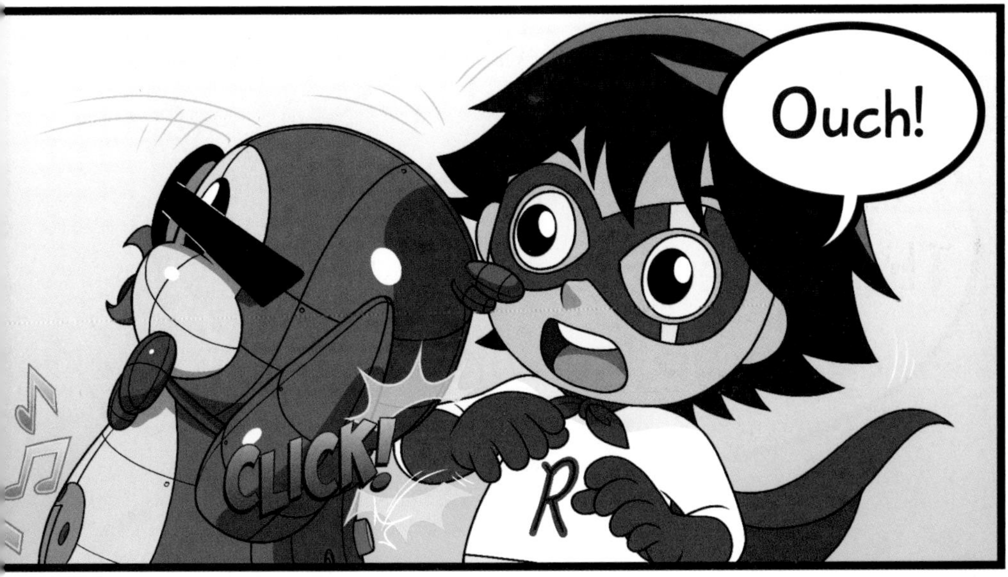
Ouch!
CLICK!

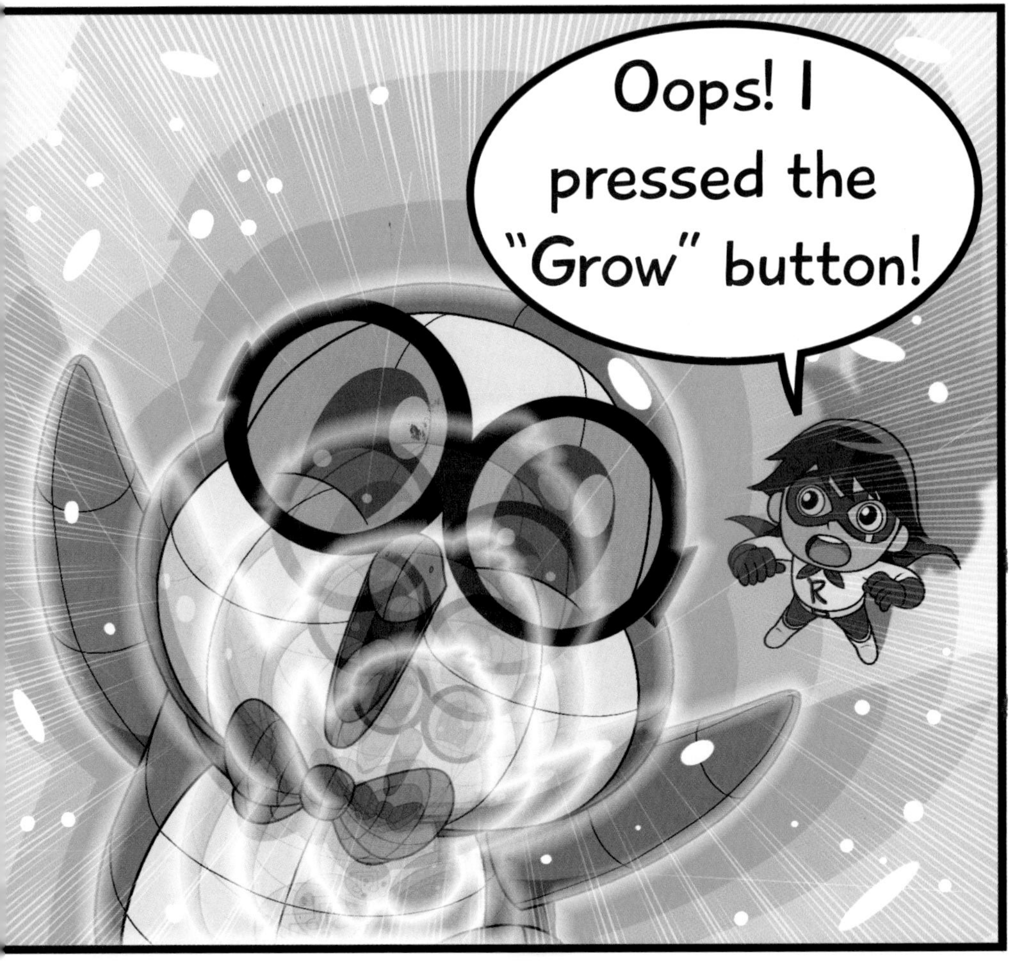
Oops! I pressed the "Grow" button!

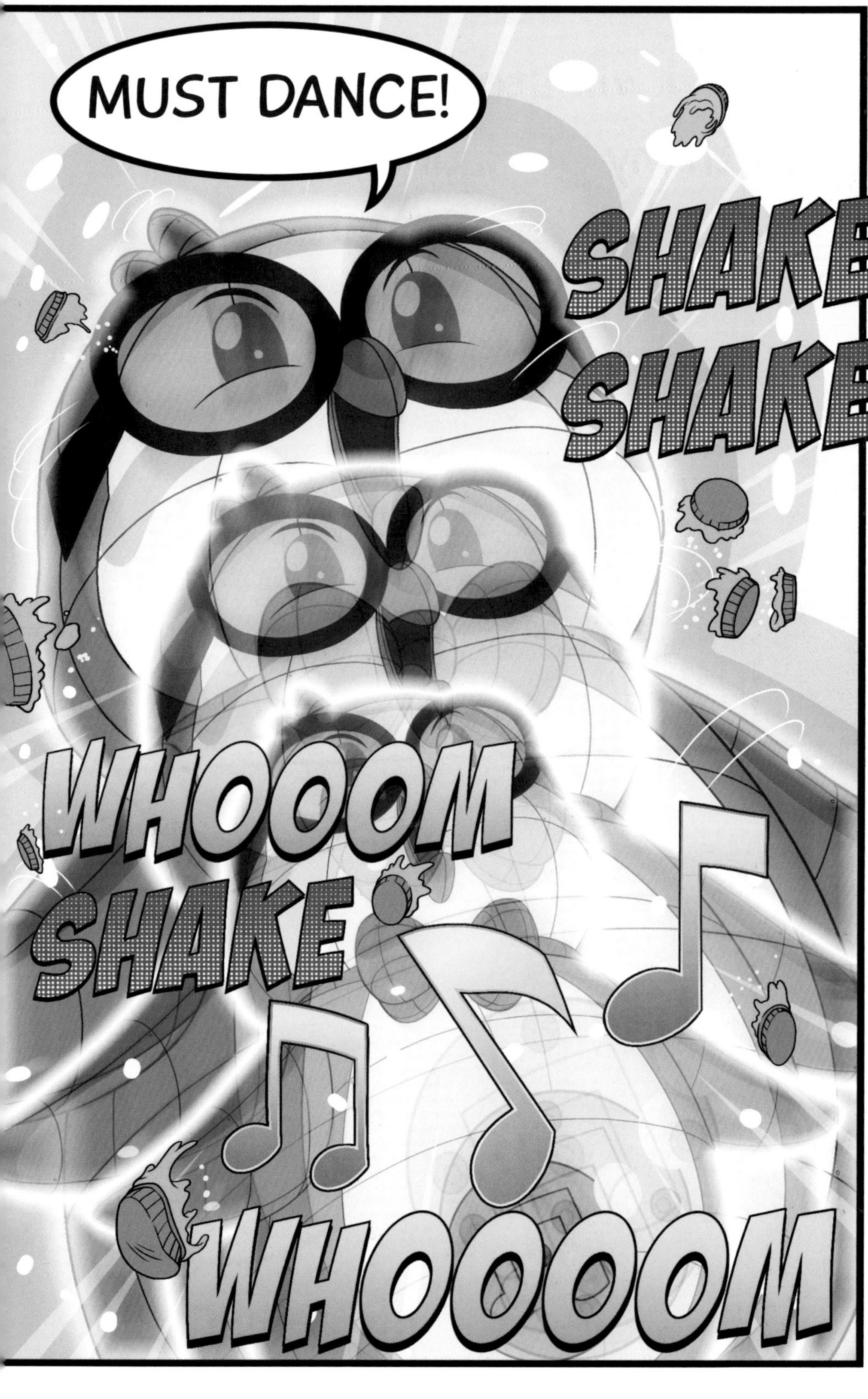
MUST DANCE!
SHAKE
SHAKE
WHOOOM
SHAKE
WHOOOOM

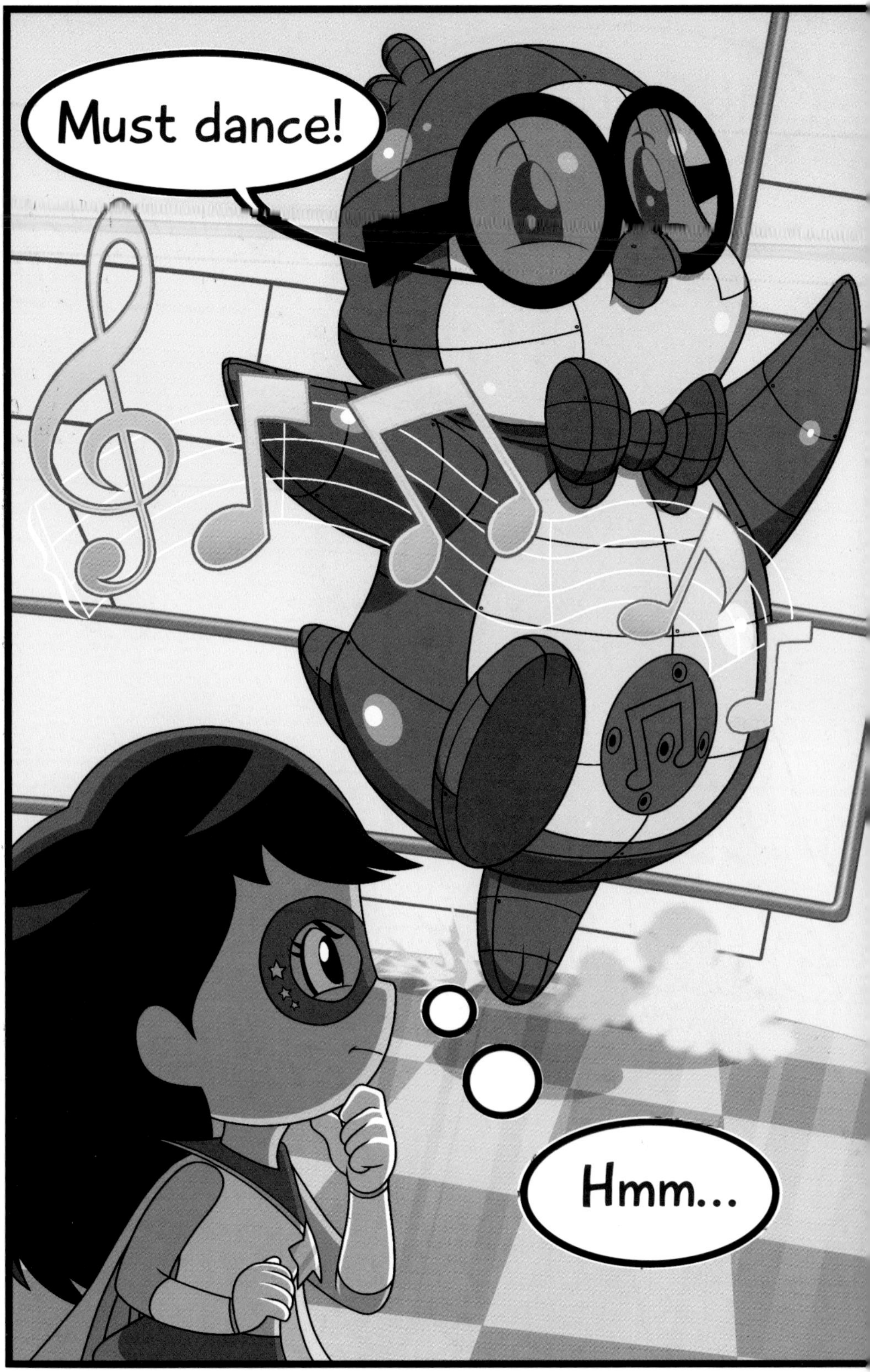
Must dance!
Hmm...

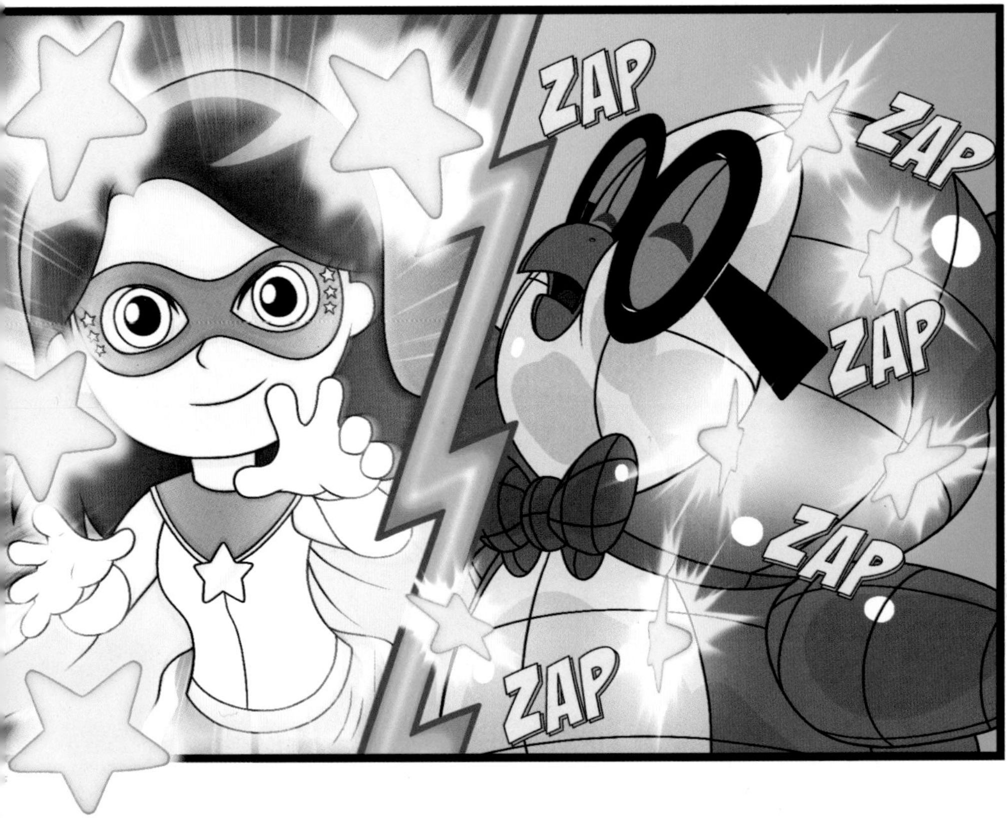
ZAP
ZAP
ZAP
ZAP
ZAP

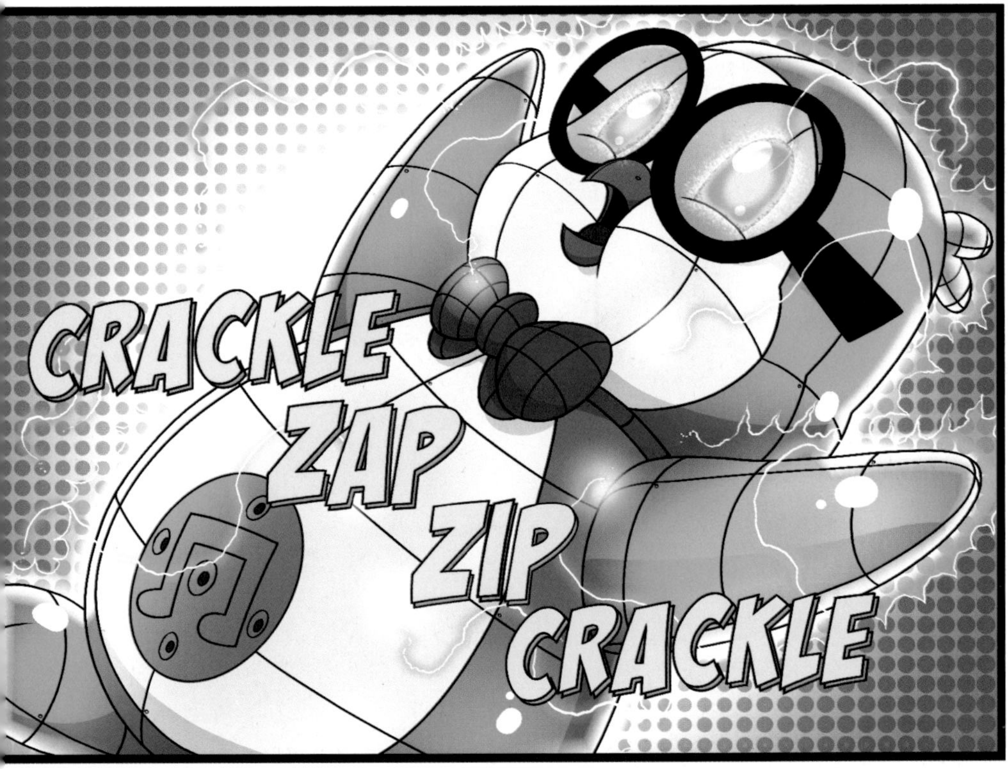
CRACKLE
ZAP
ZIP
CRACKLE

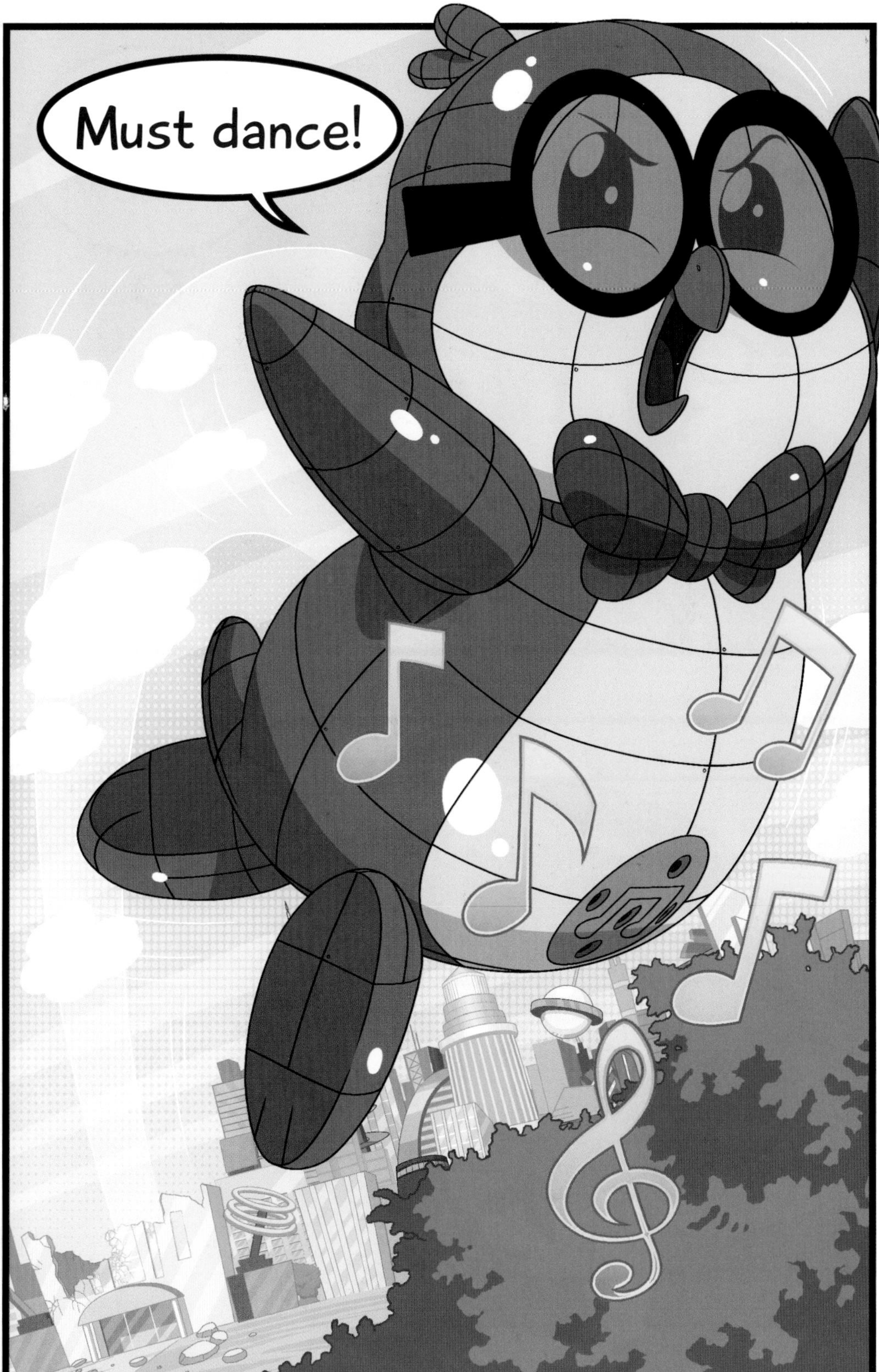
Must dance!

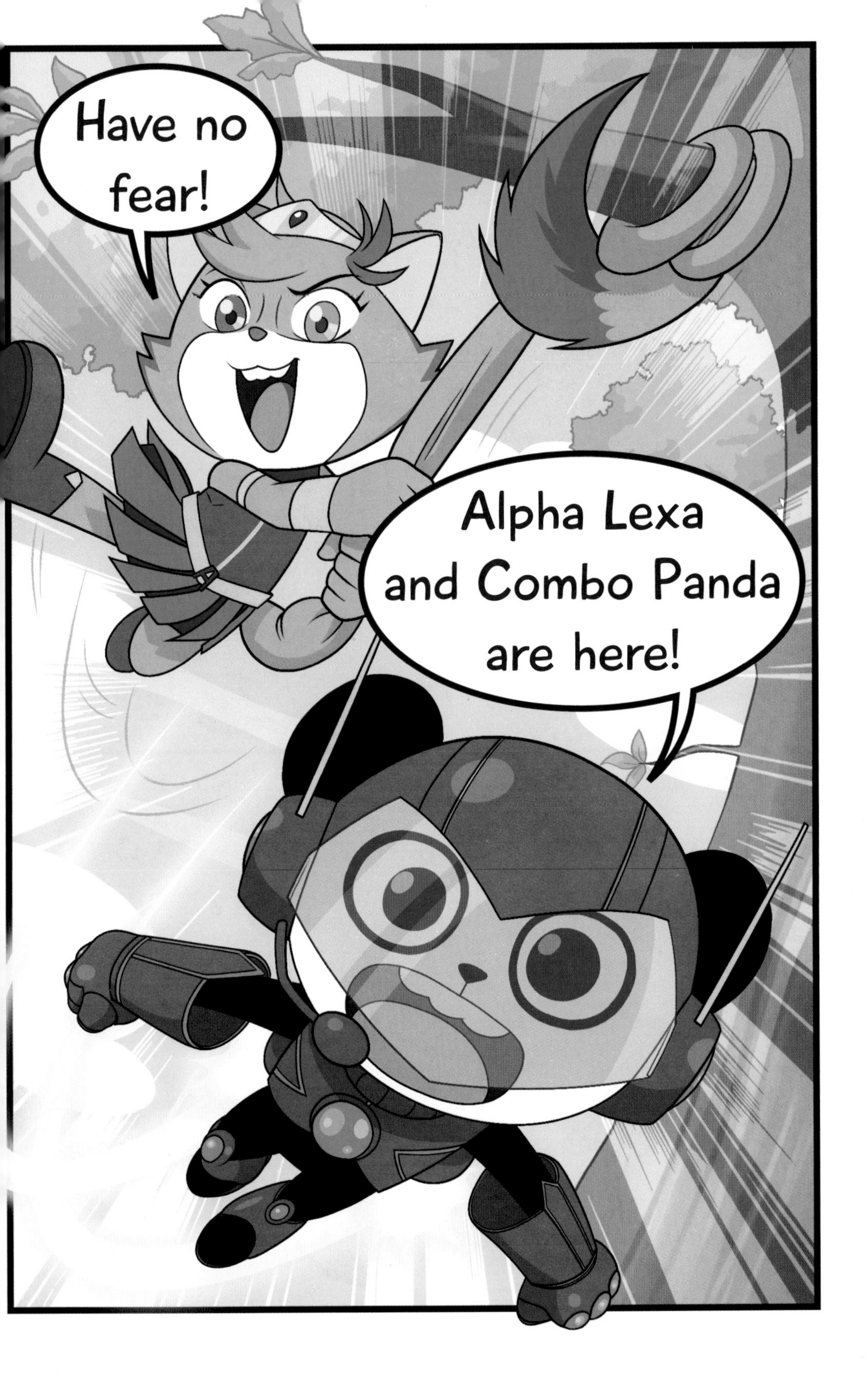
Have no fear!
Alpha Lexa and Combo Panda are here!

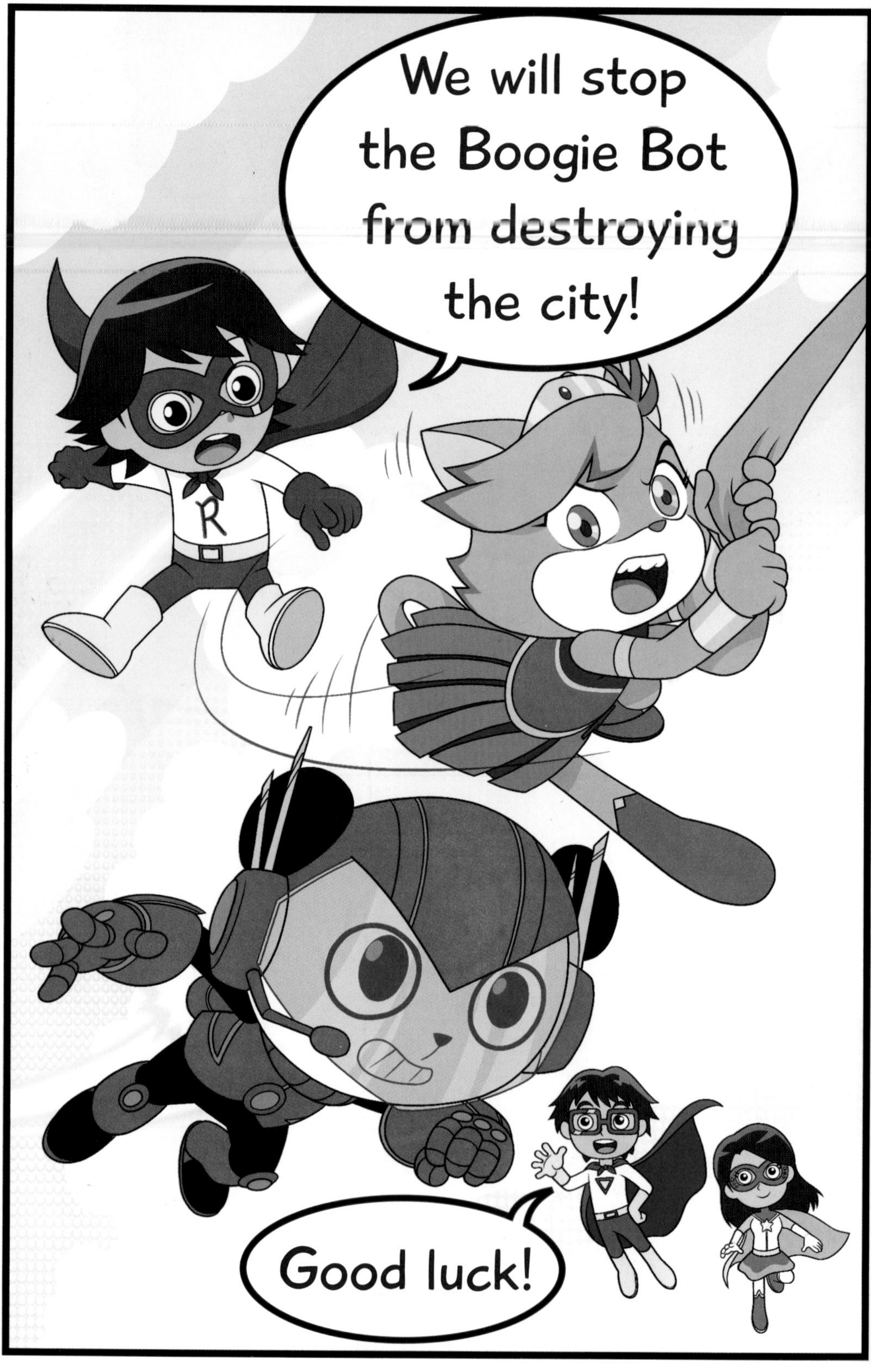
We will stop the Boogie Bot from destroying the city!
Good luck!

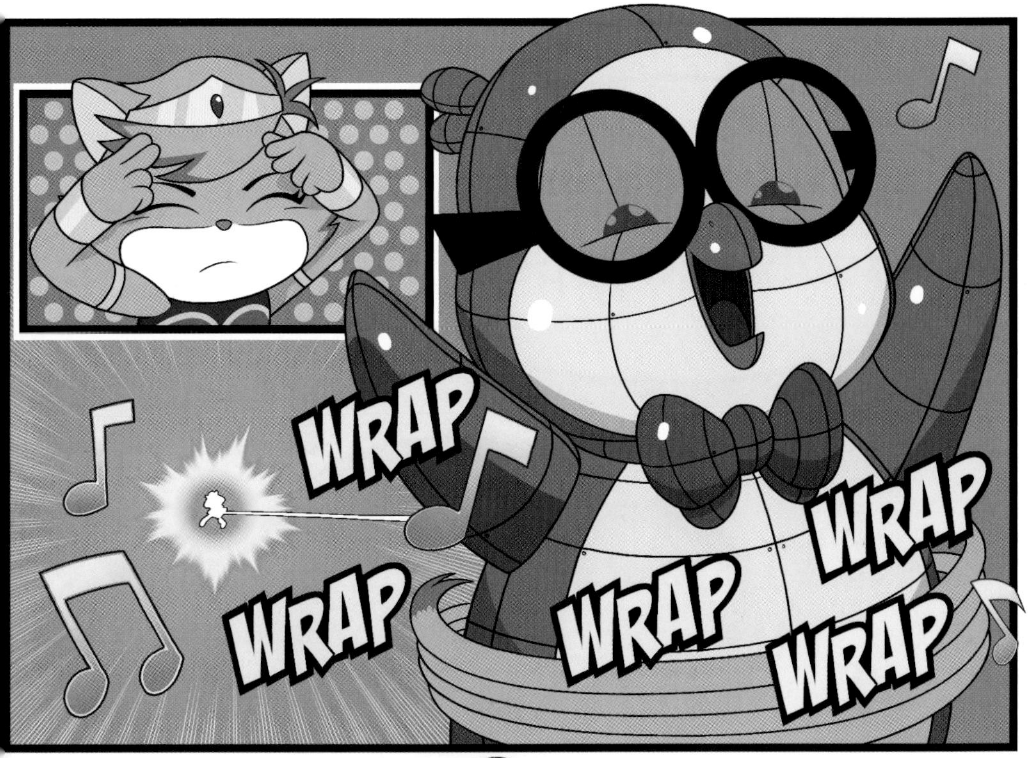
WRAP
WRAP
WRAP
WRAP
WRAP

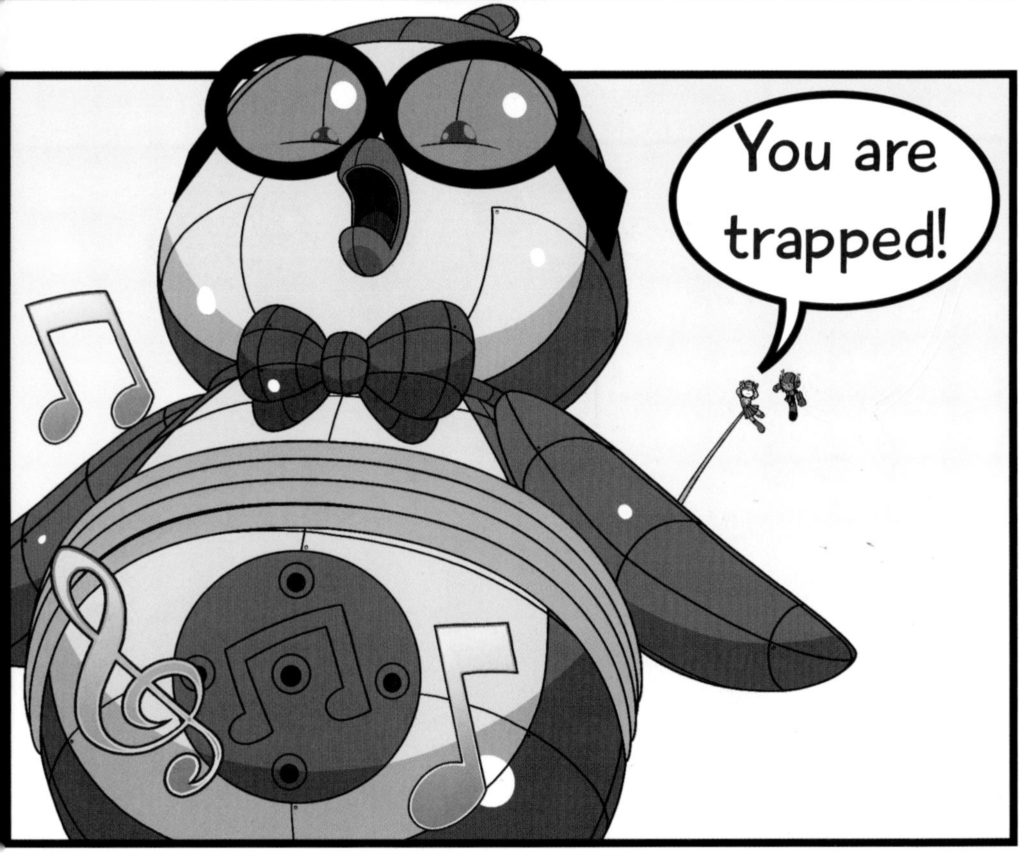
You are trapped!

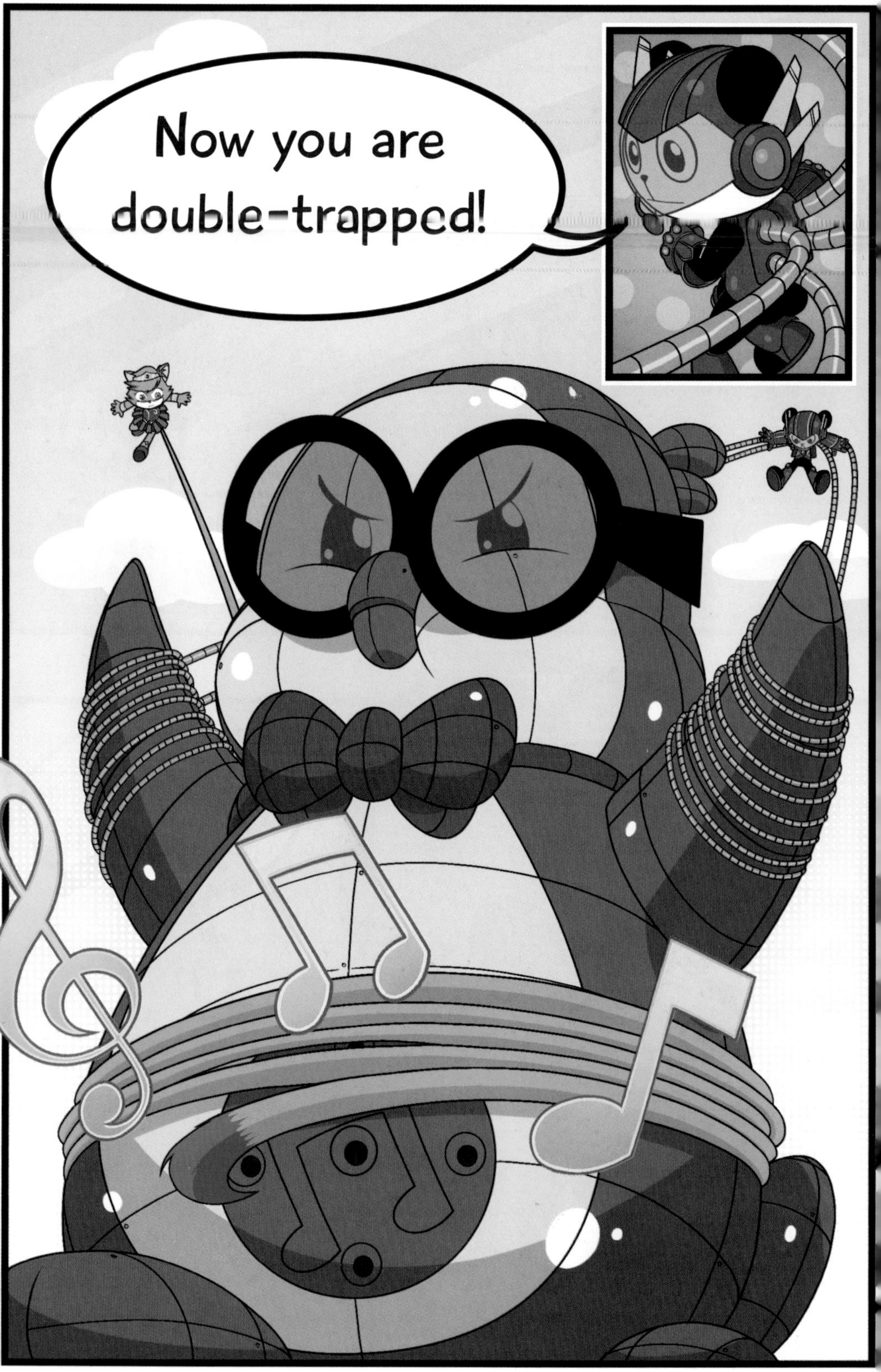
Now you are double-trapped!

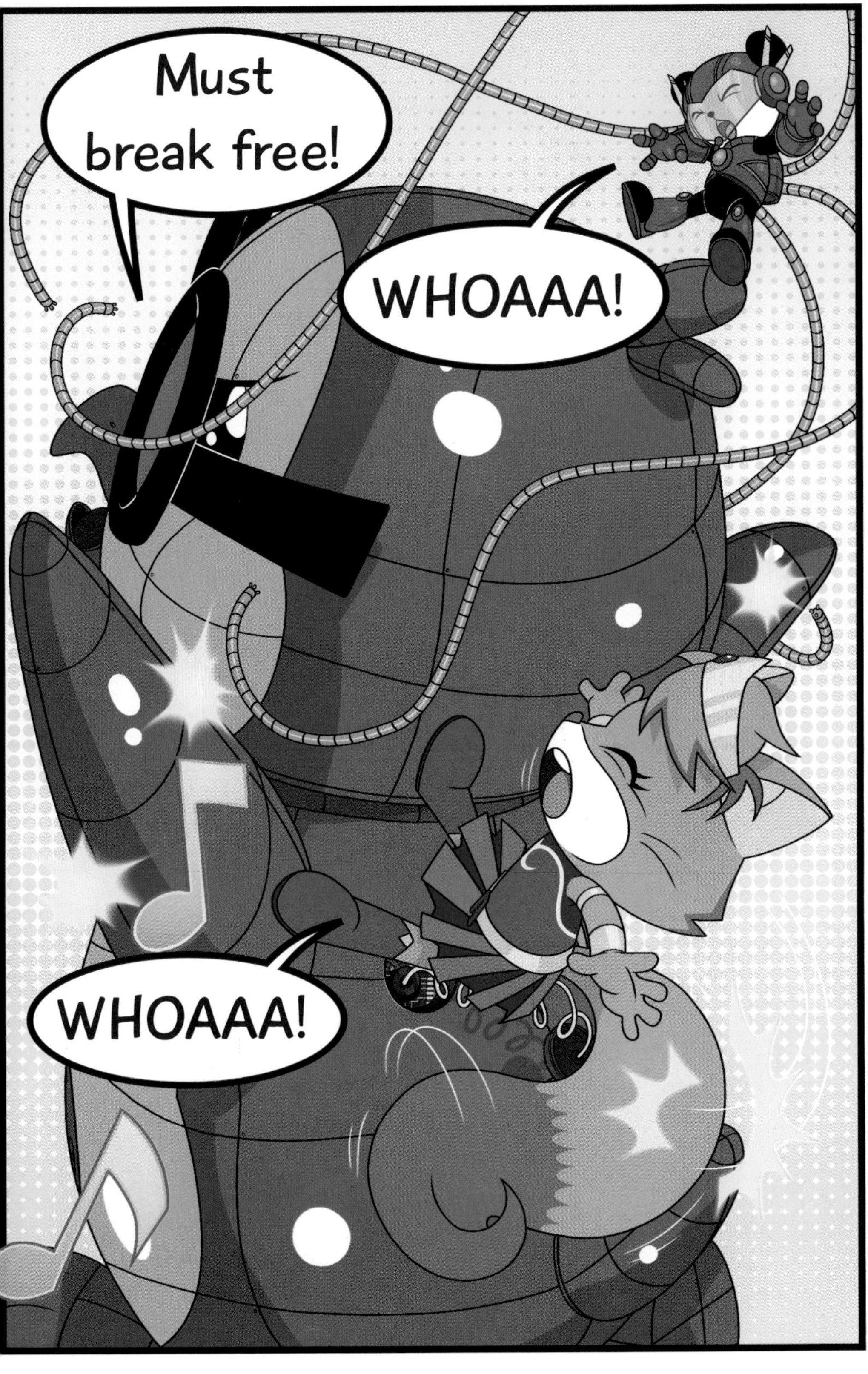
Must break free!
WHOAAA!
WHOAAA!

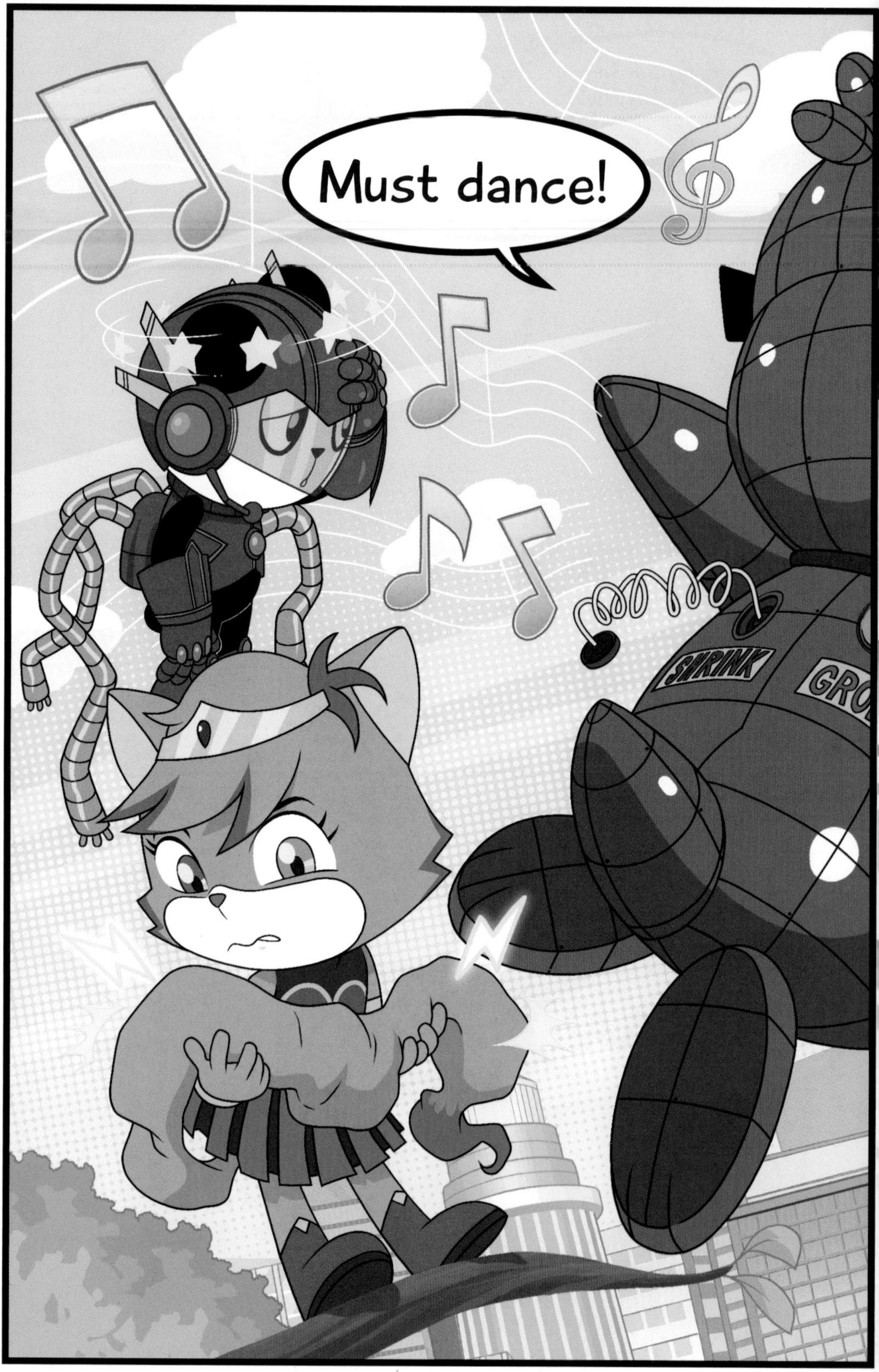
Must dance!
SHRINK

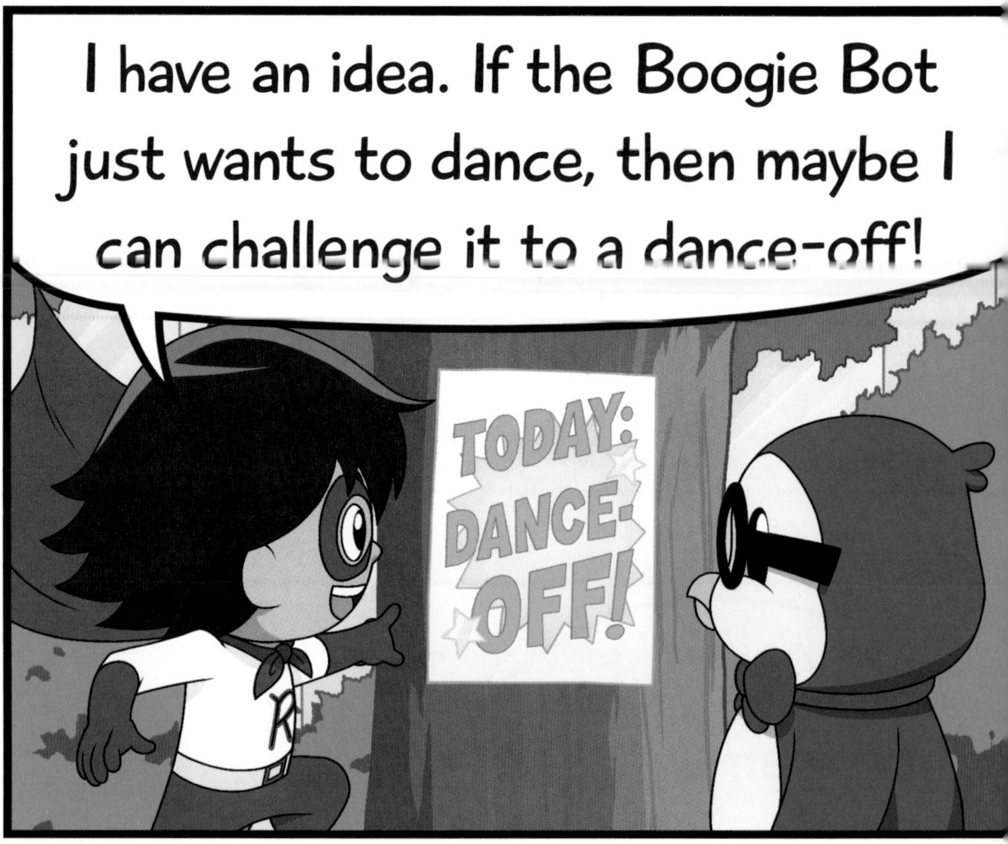
I have an idea. If the Boogie Bot just wants to dance, then maybe I can challenge it to a dance-off!
TODAY: DANCE-OFF!

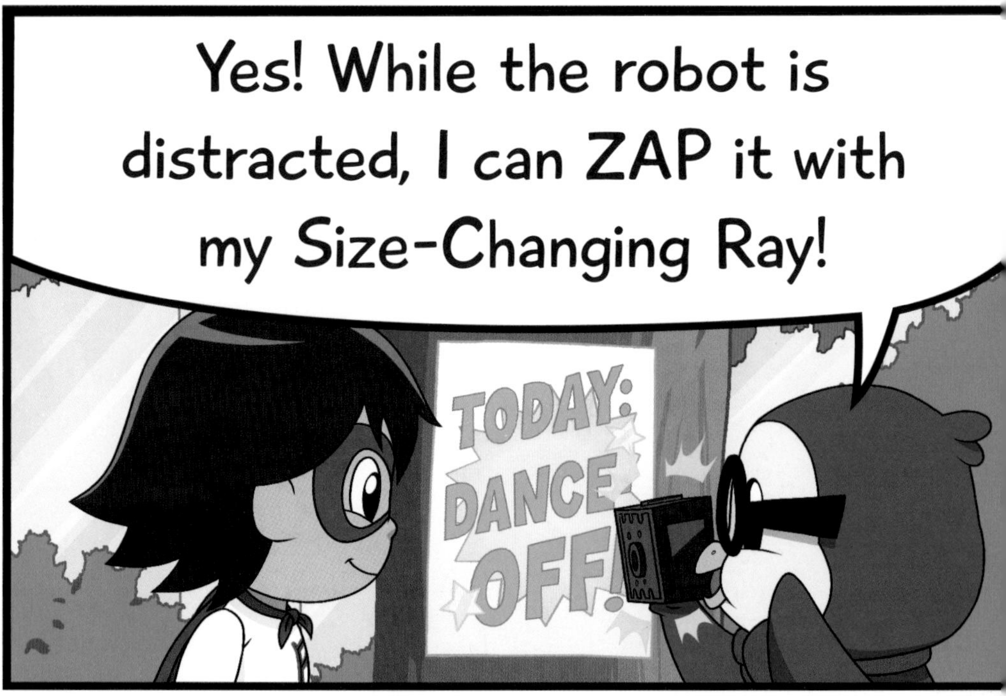
Yes! While the robot is distracted, I can ZAP it with my Size-Changing Ray!
TODAY: DANCE-OFF!

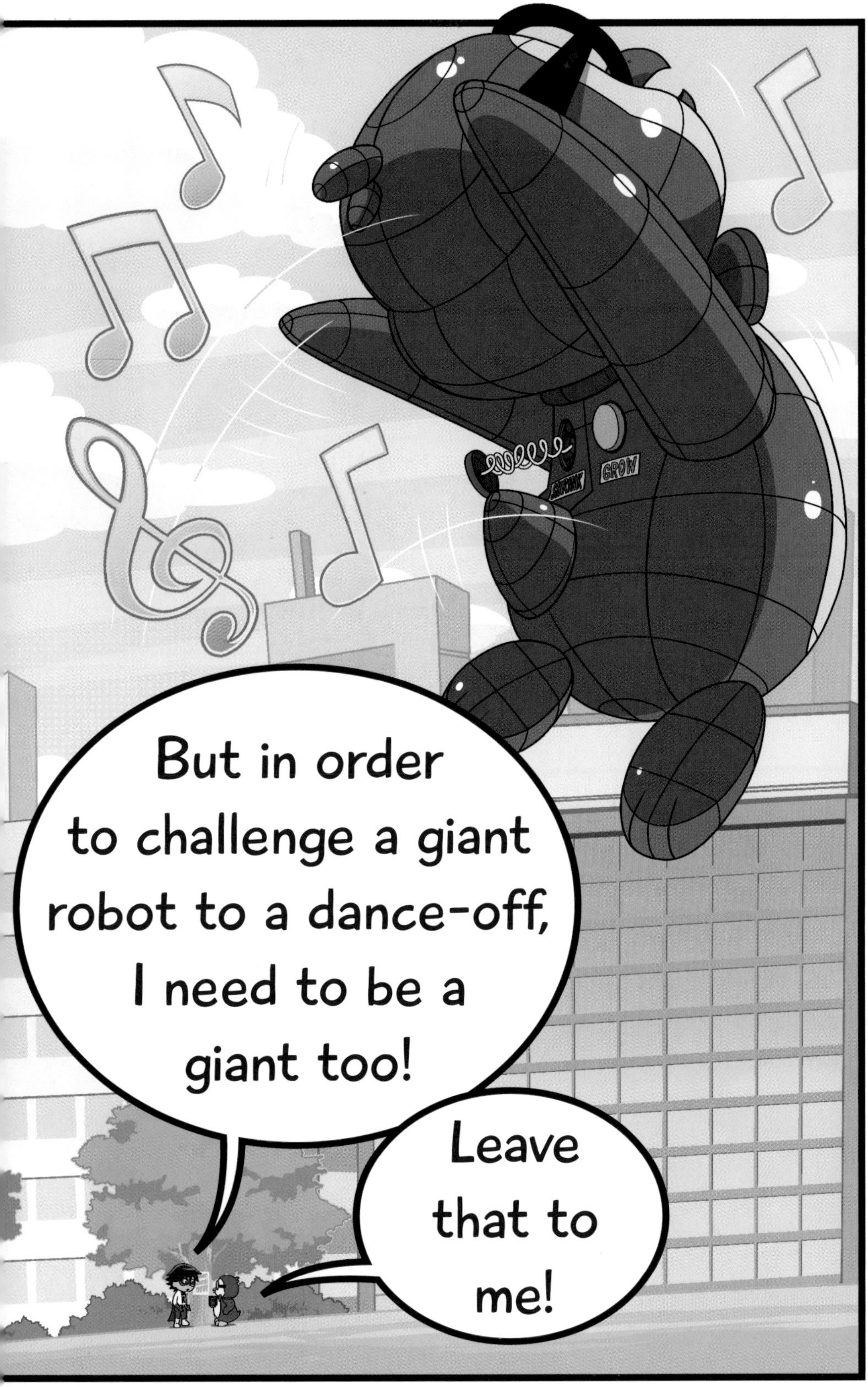
SHRINK
GROW
But in order to challenge a giant robot to a dance-off, I need to be a giant too!
Leave that to me!

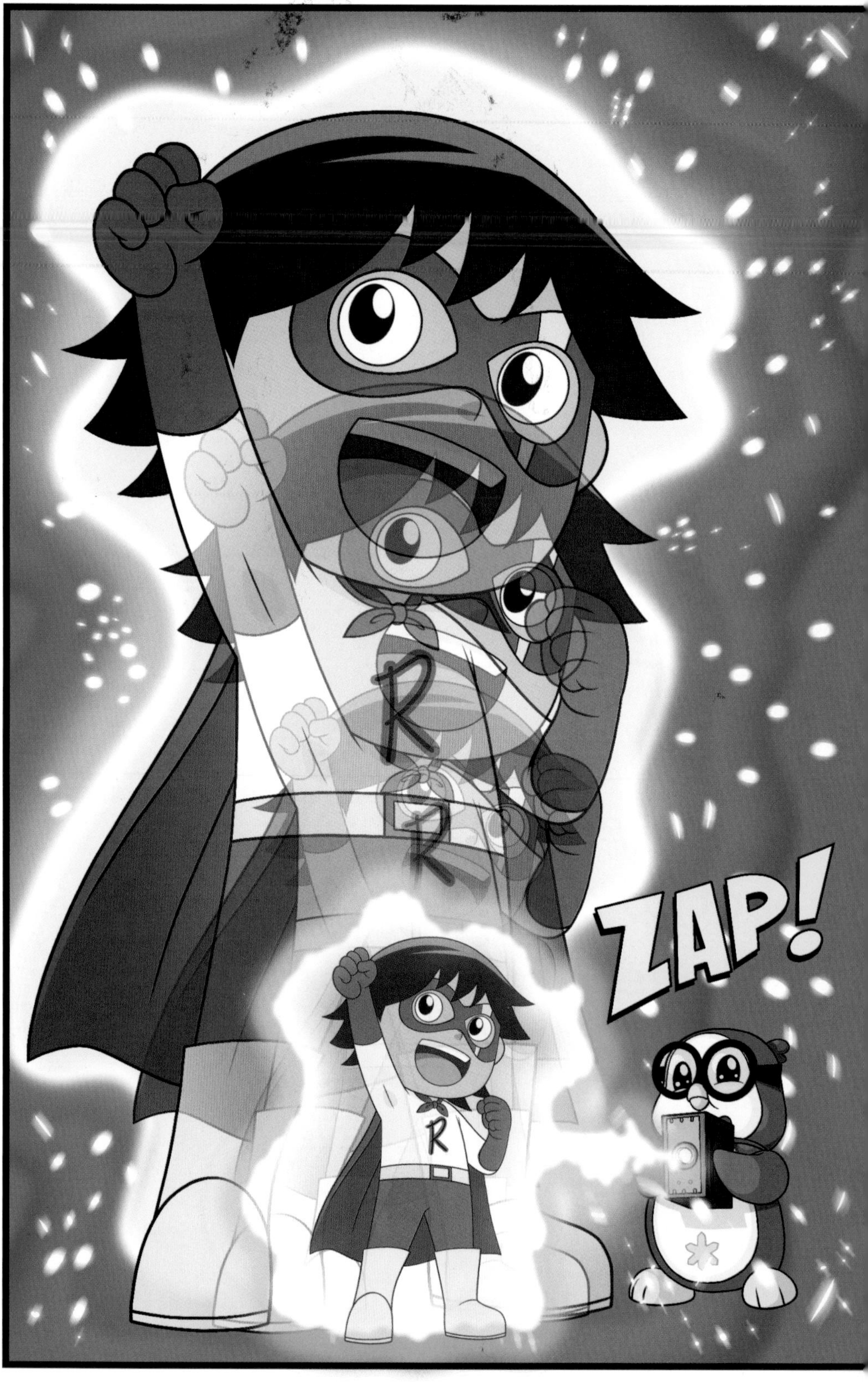
ZAP!

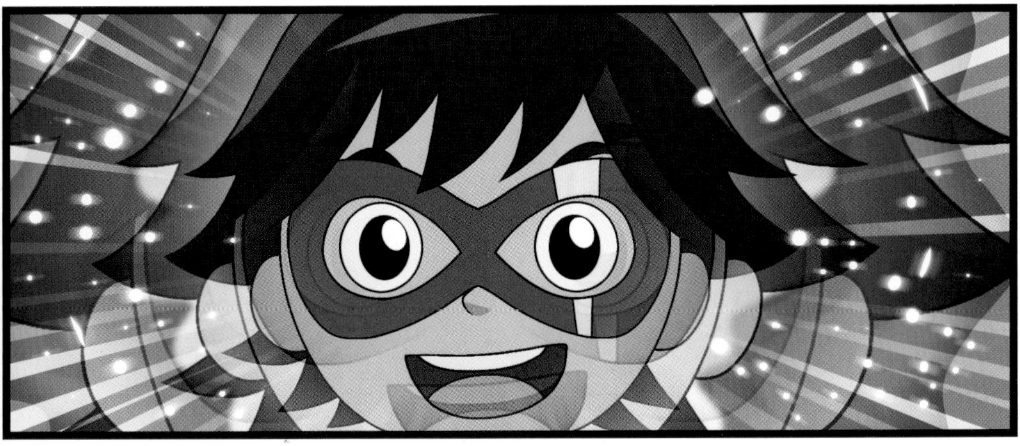

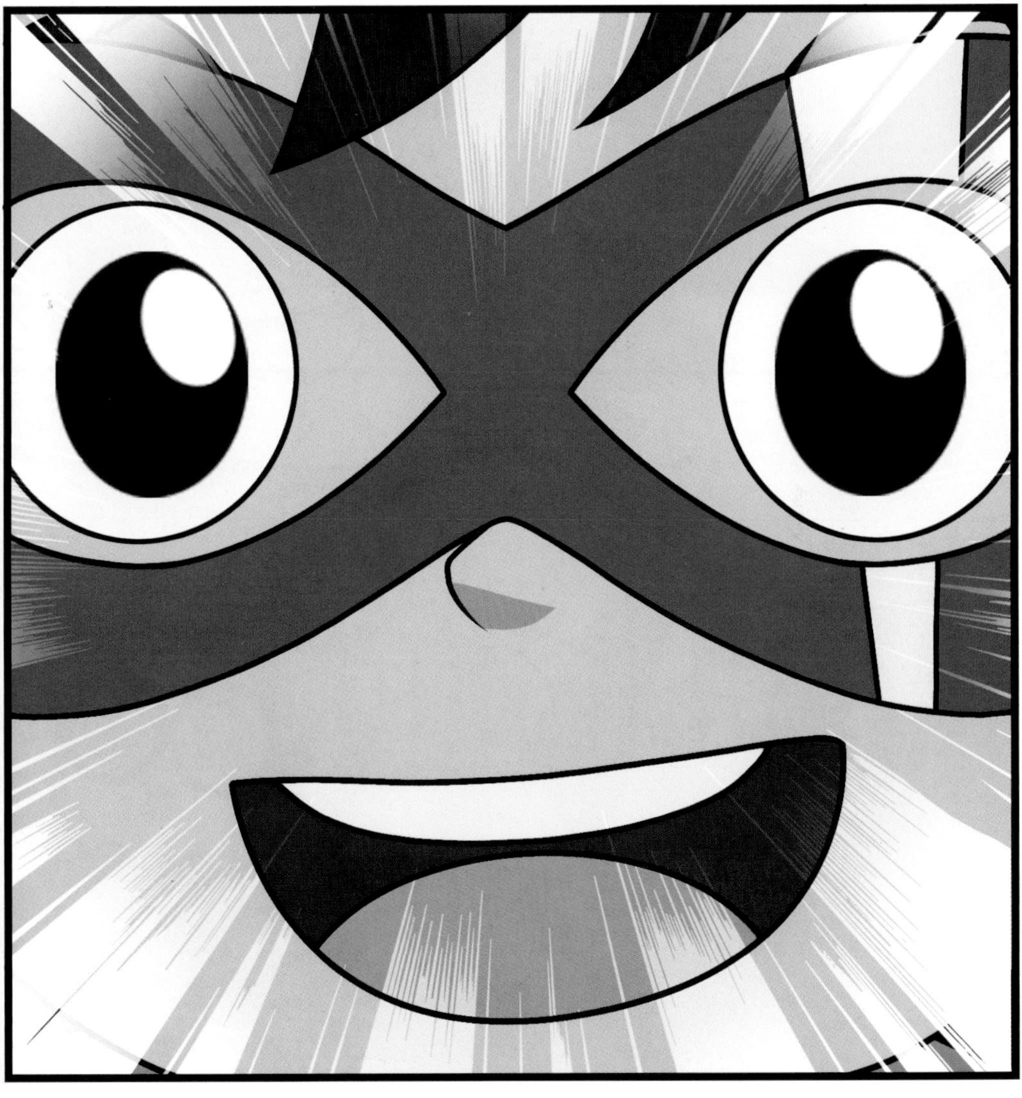

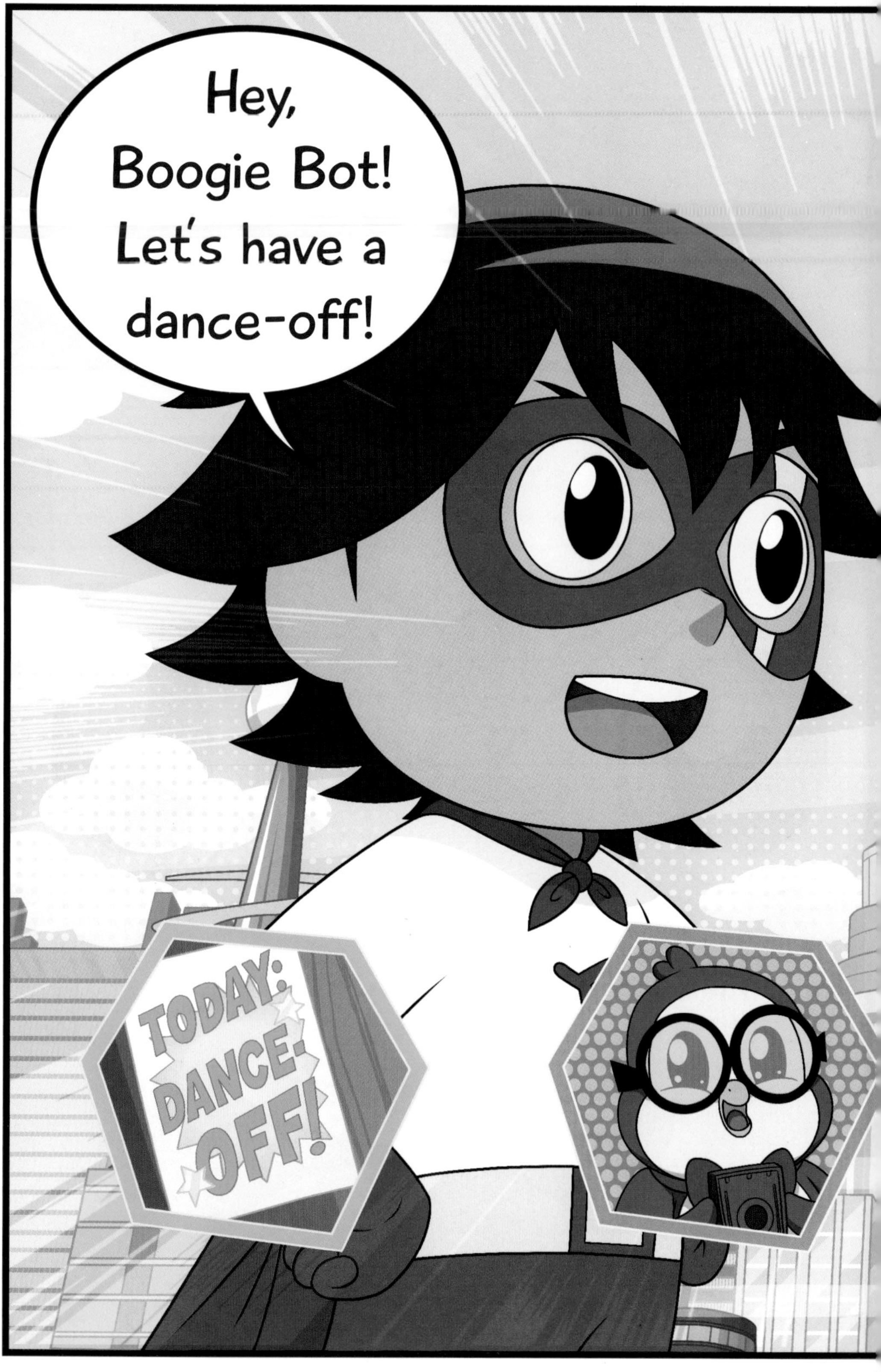
Hey, Boogie Bot! Let's have a dance-off!
TODAY: DANCE-OFF!

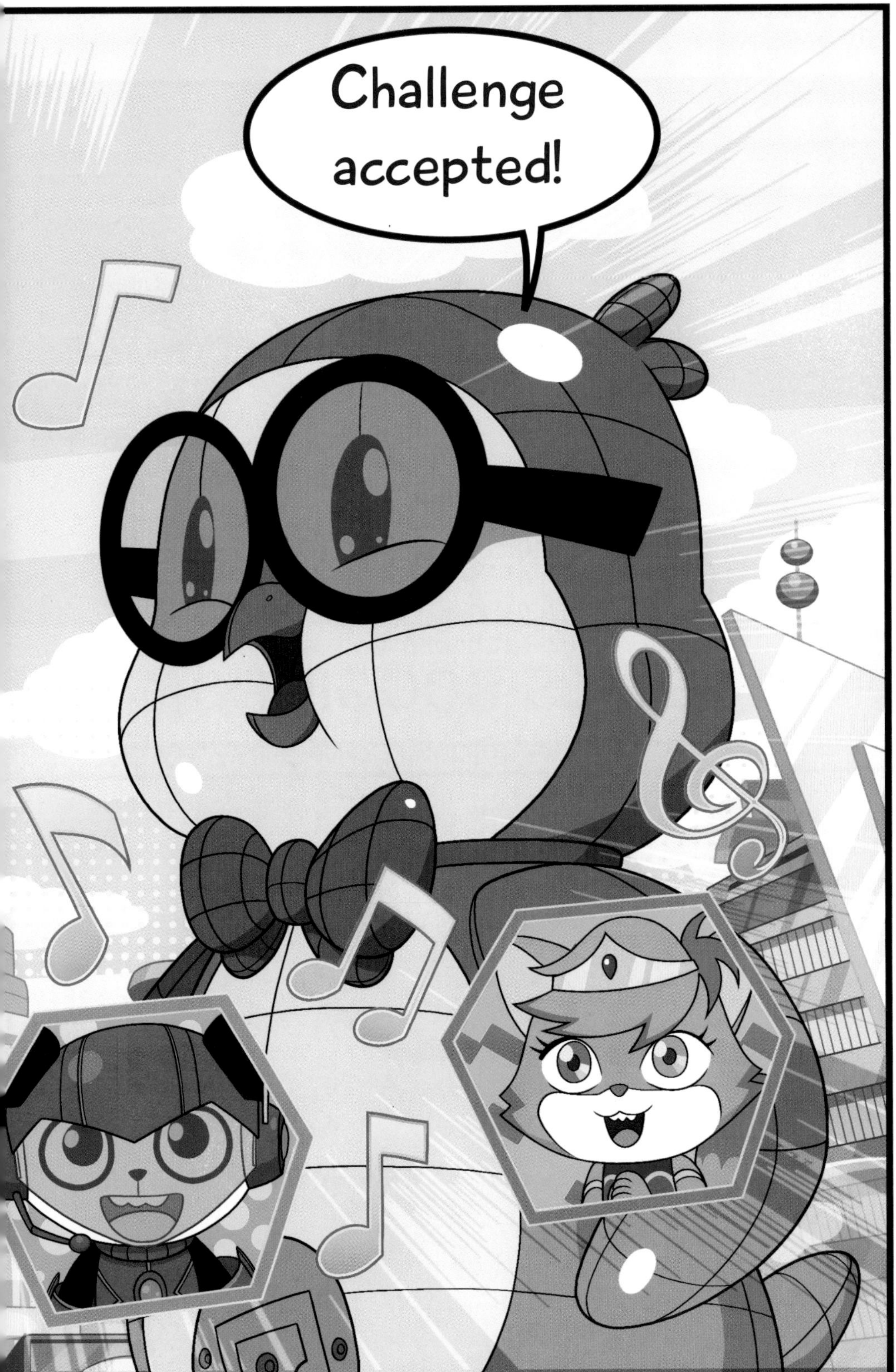
Challenge accepted!

RED TITAN

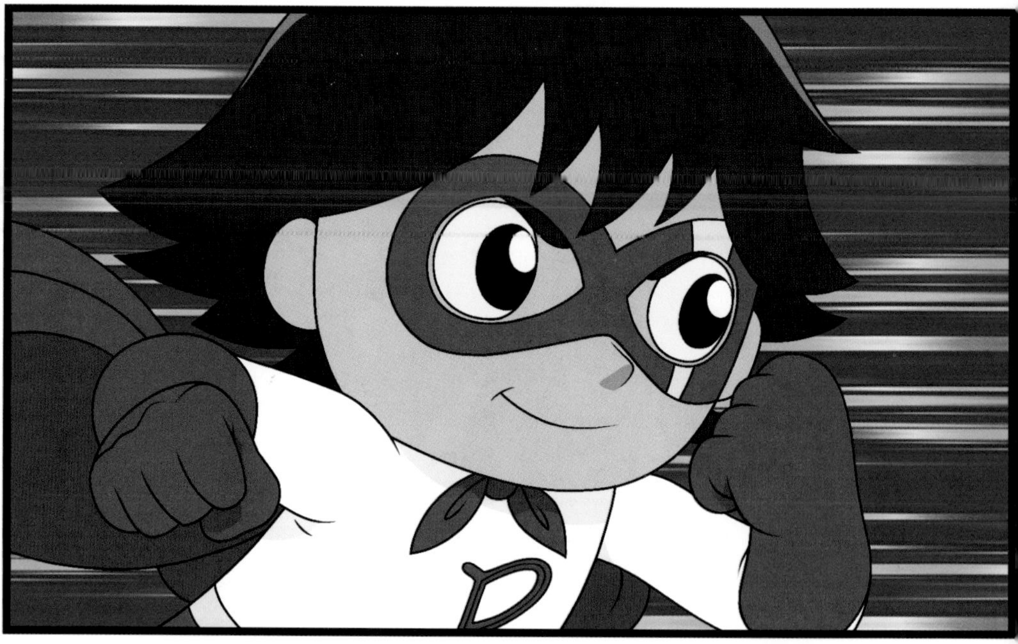

VERSUS BOOGIE BOT

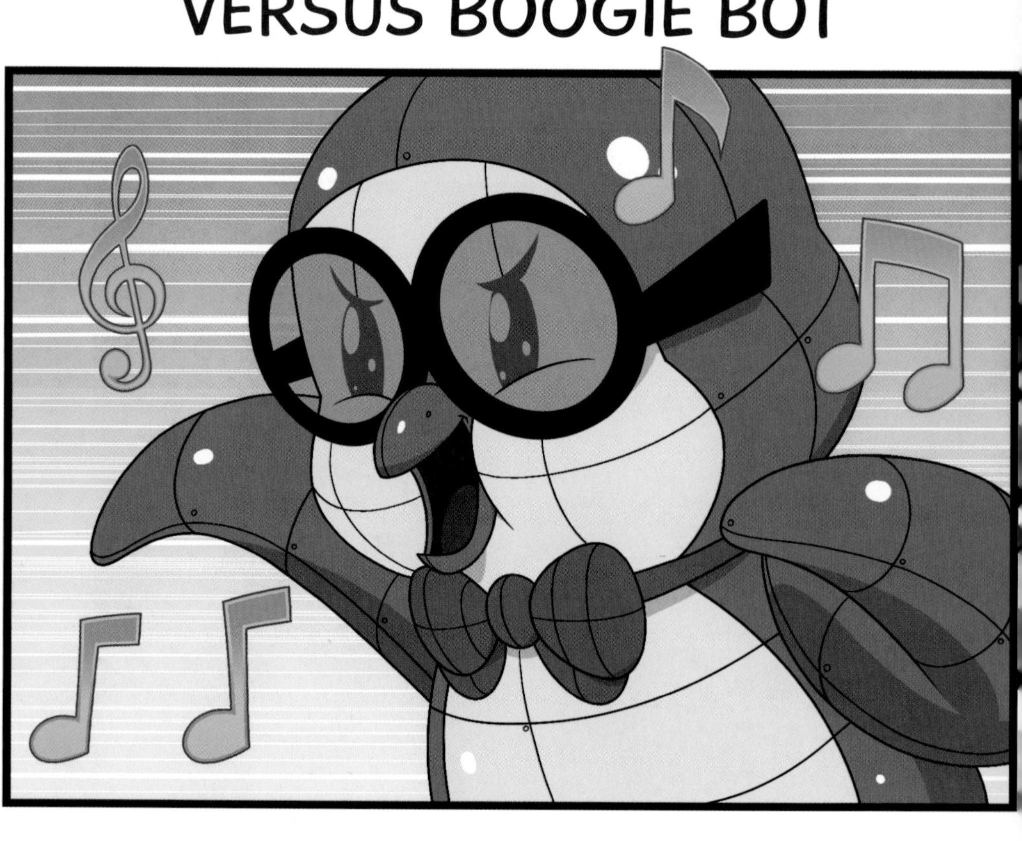

BEGIN!

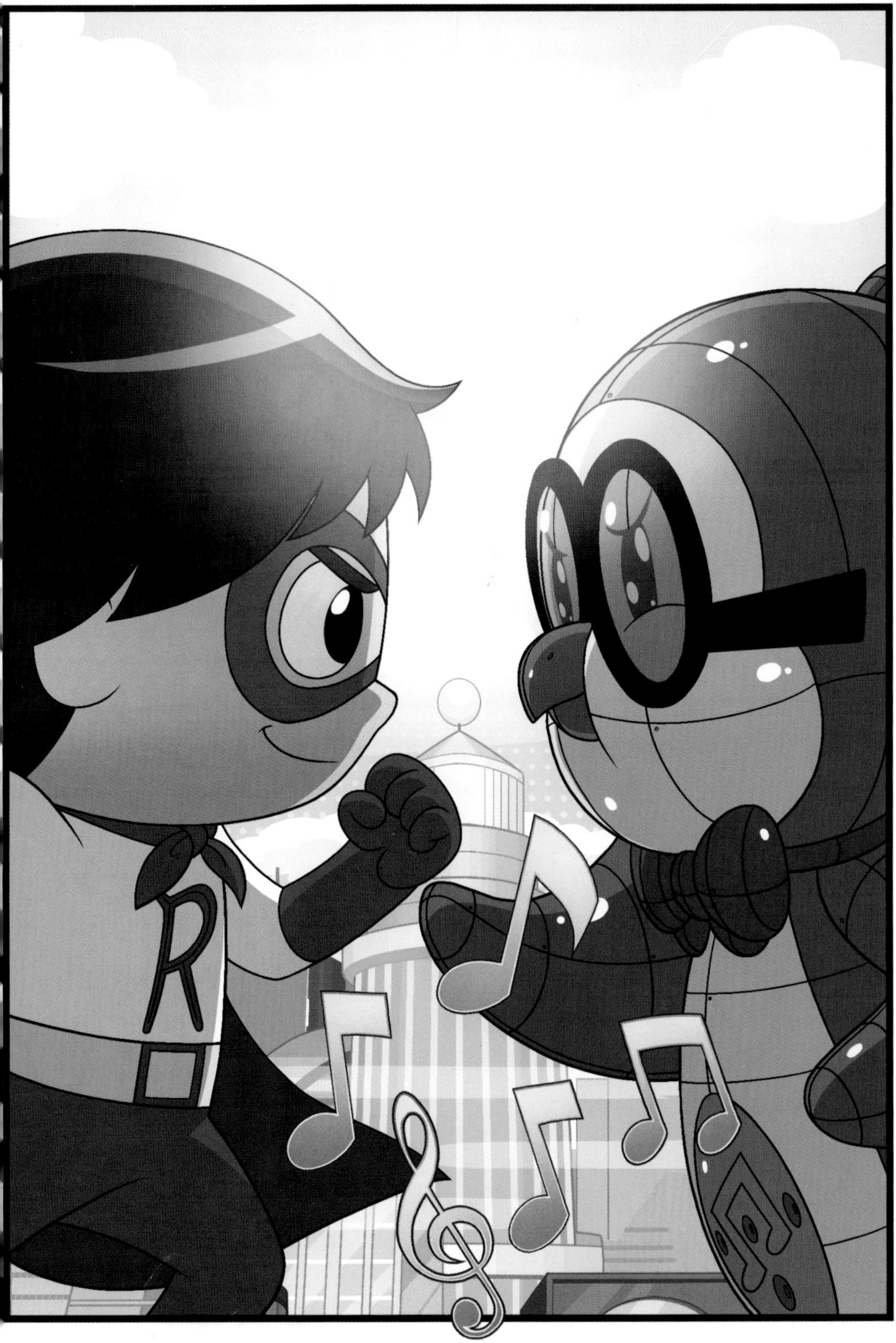

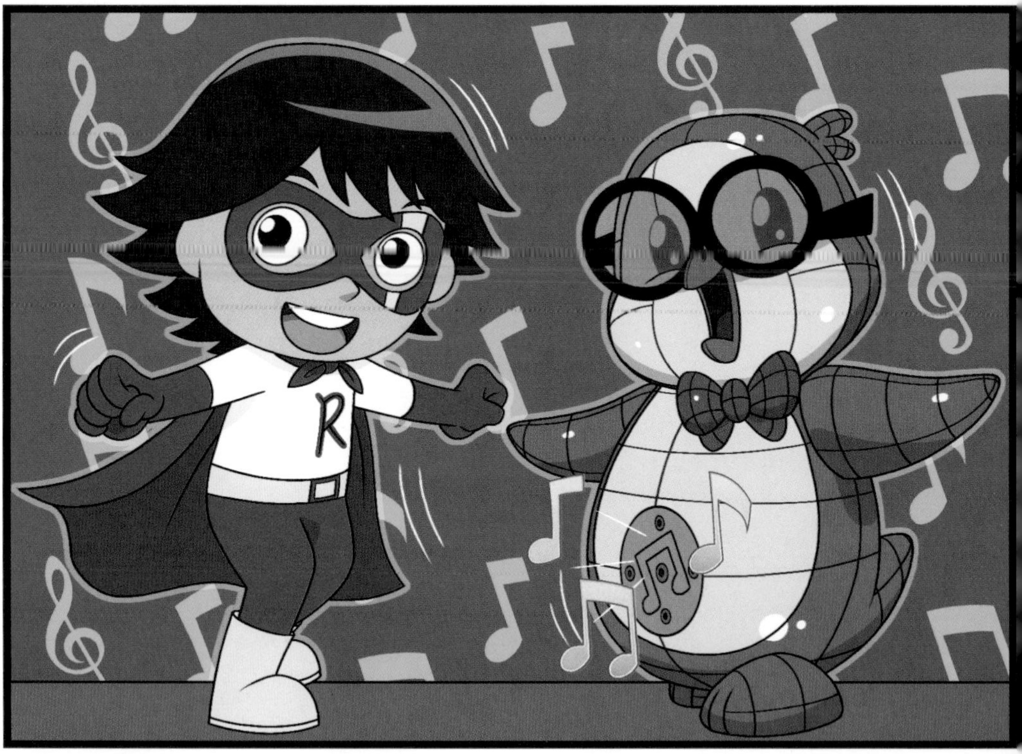

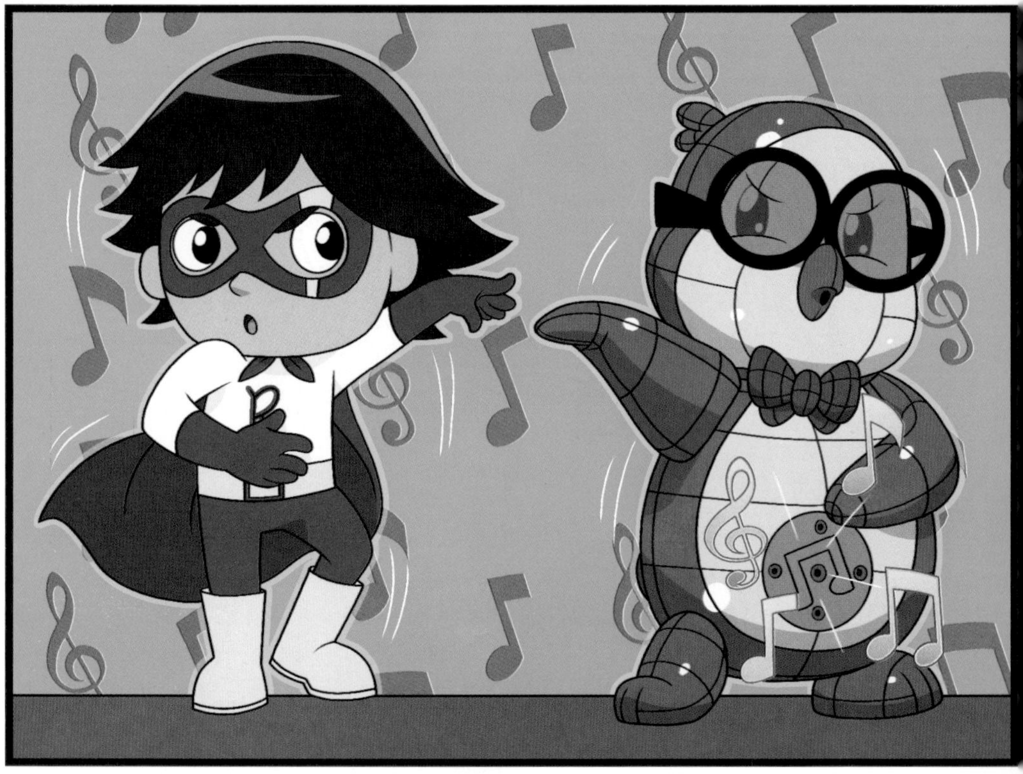

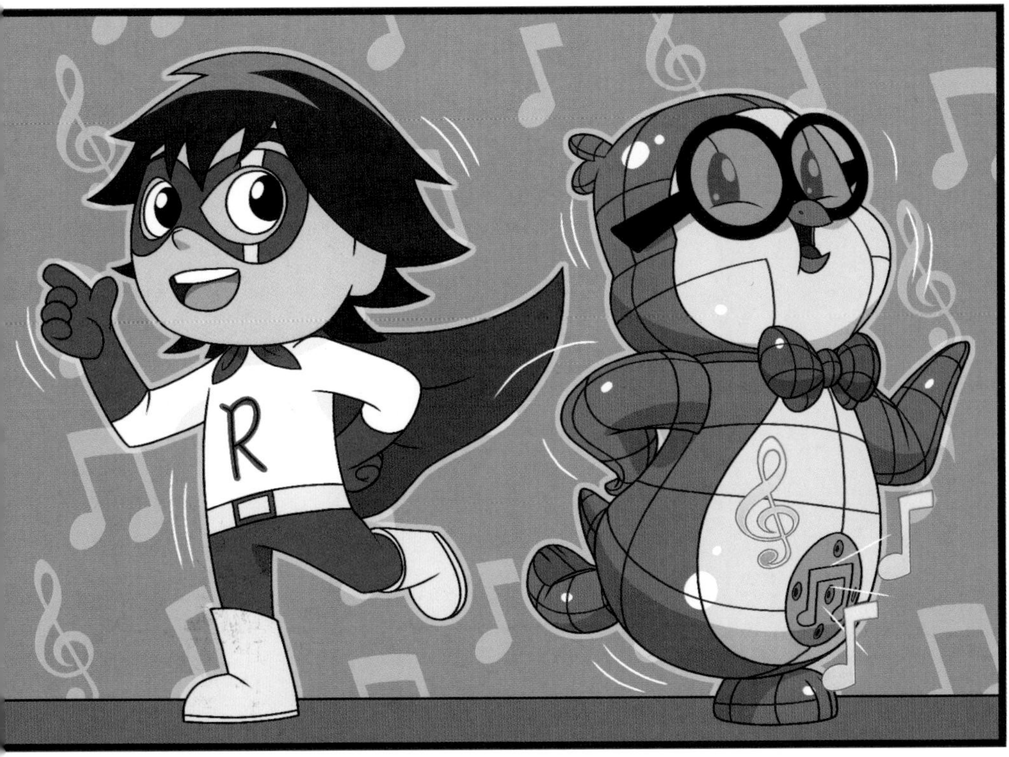

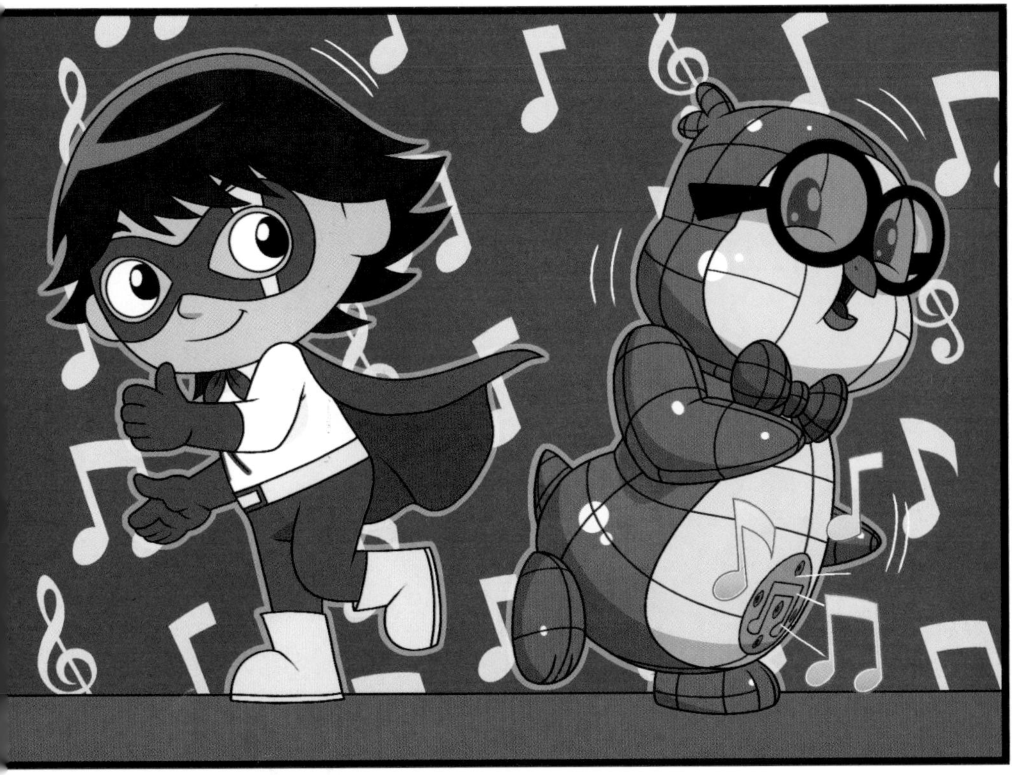

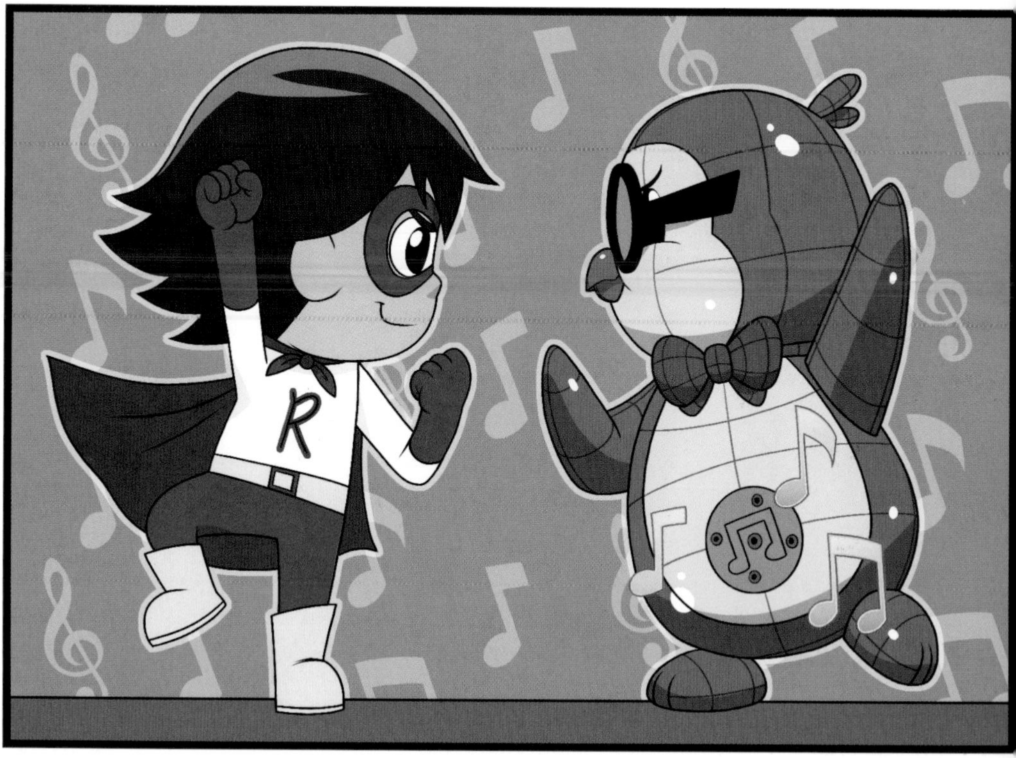

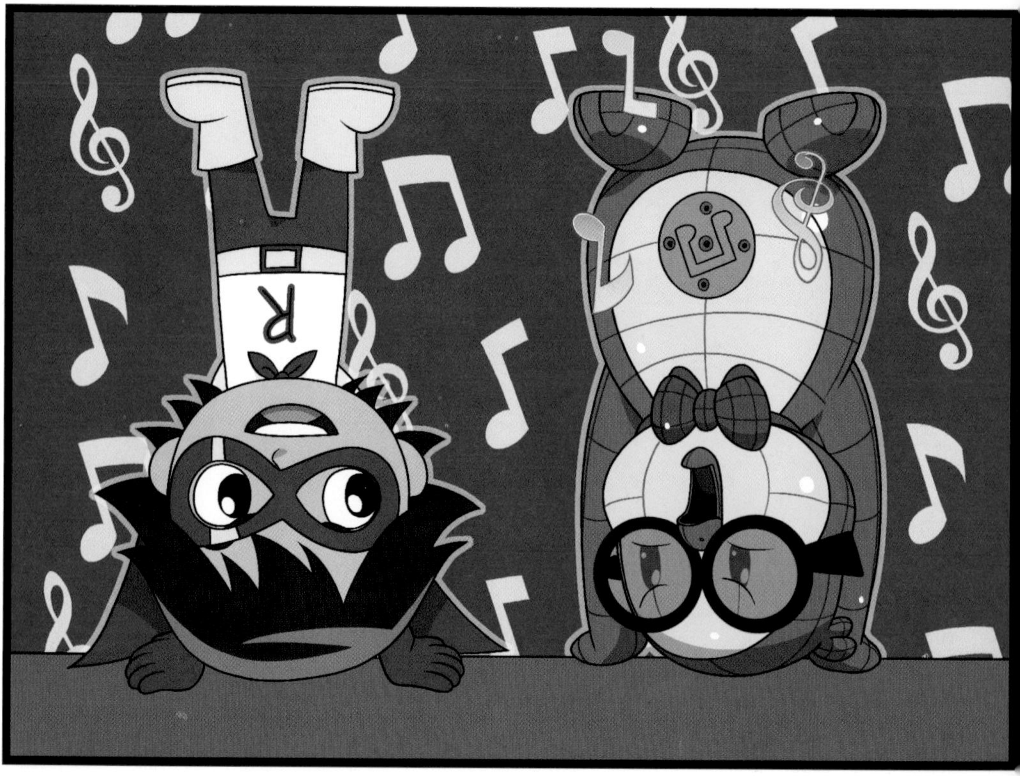

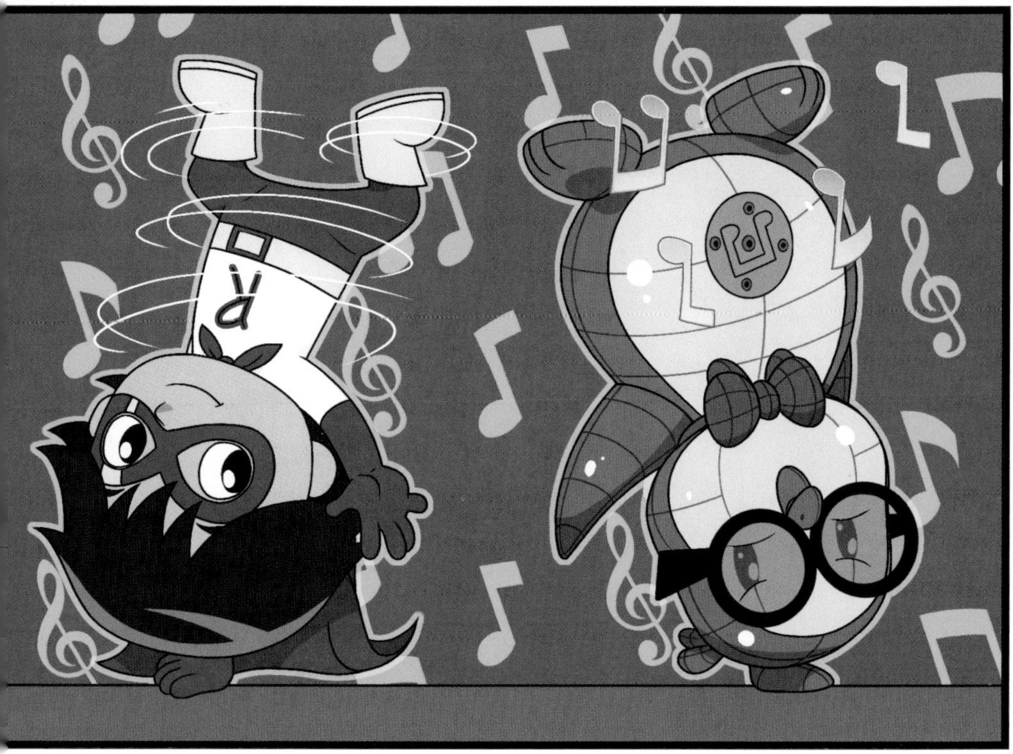

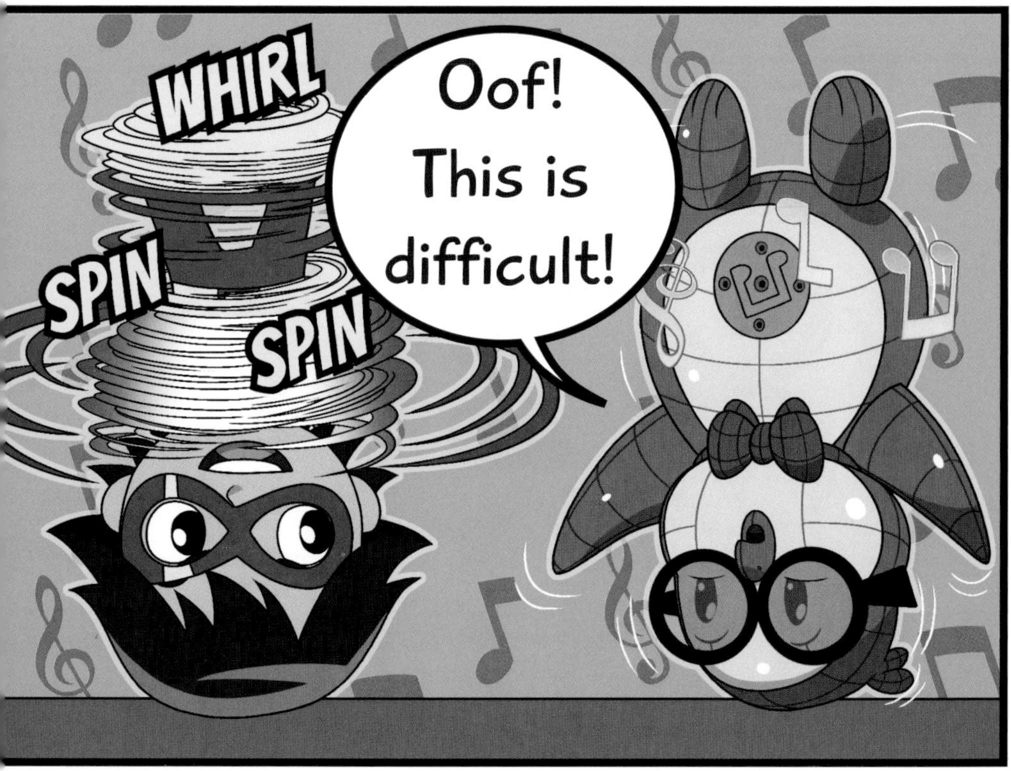
WHIRL
SPIN
SPIN
Oof! This is difficult!

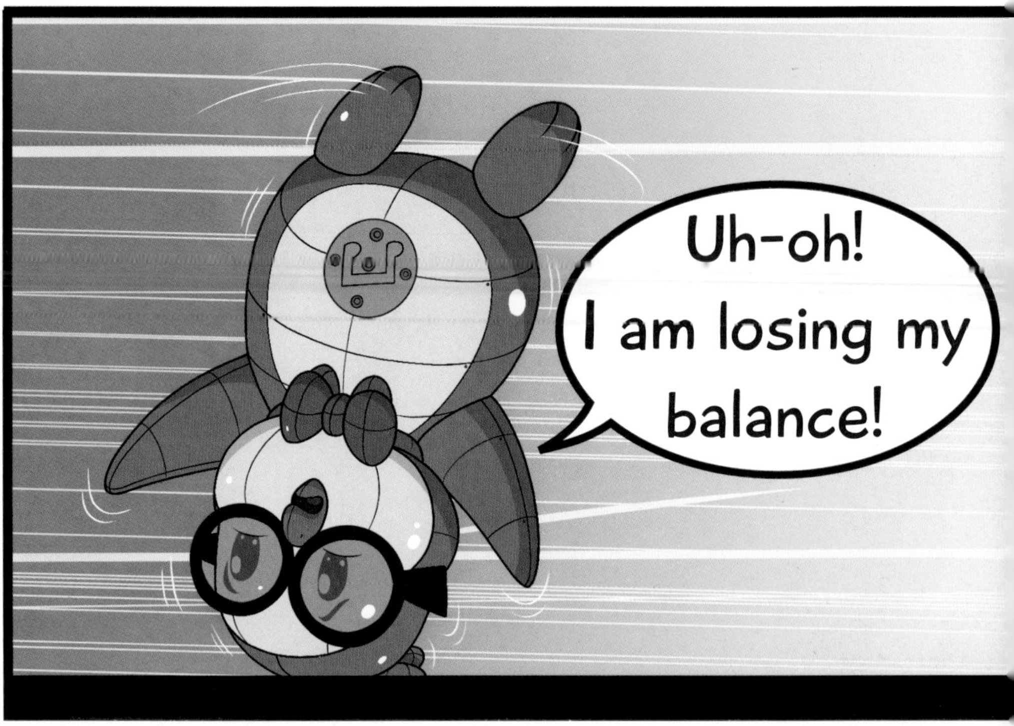
Uh-oh!
I am losing my
balance!

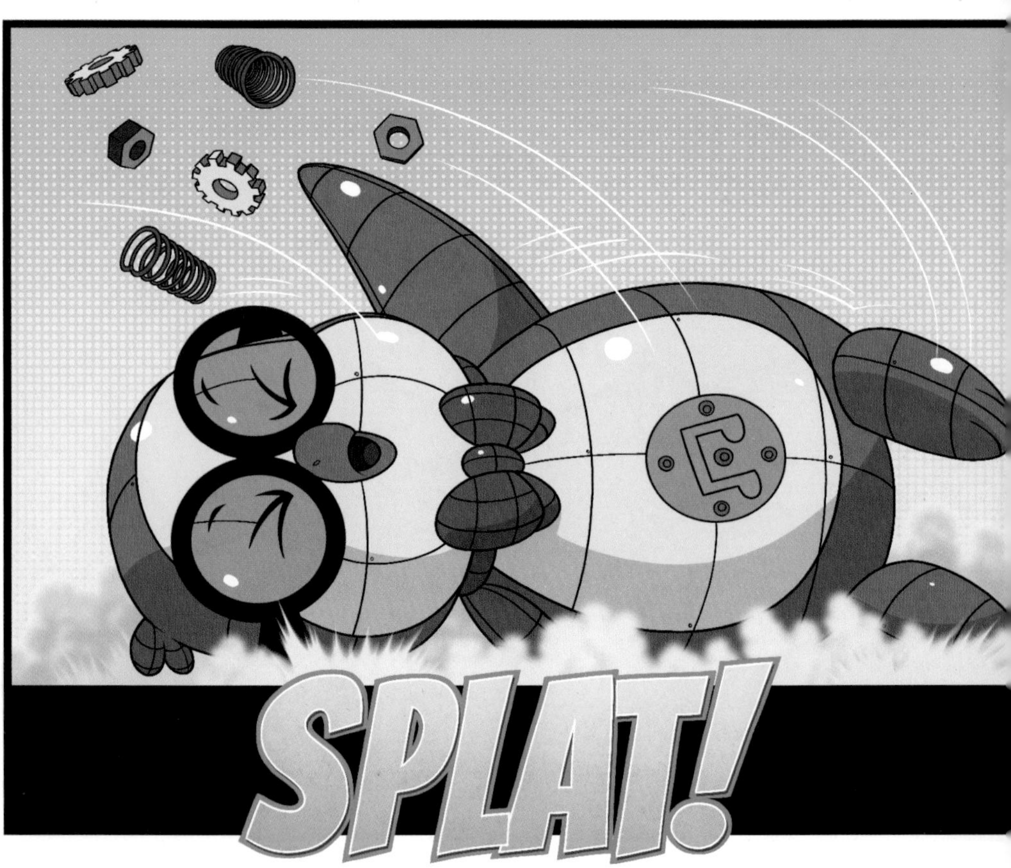
SPLAT!

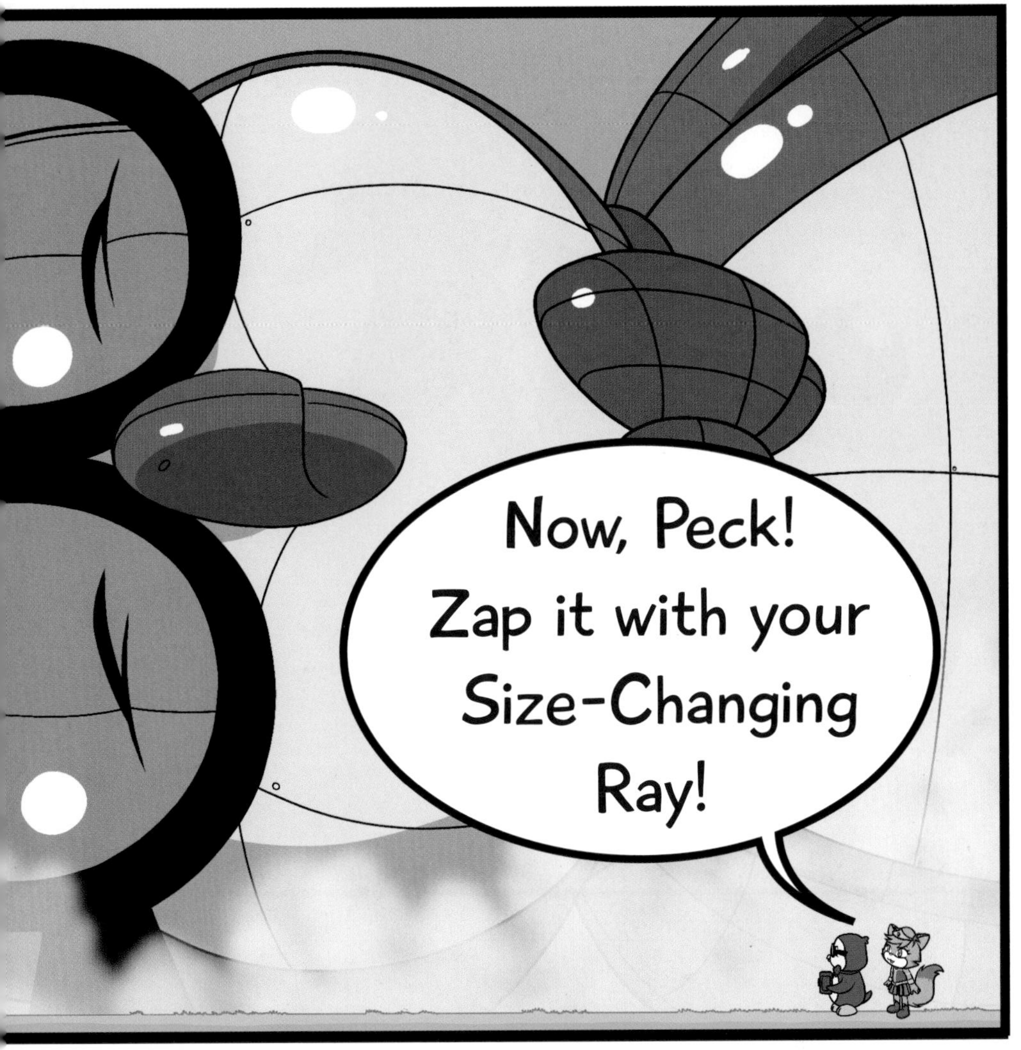
Now, Peck! Zap it with your Size-Changing Ray!

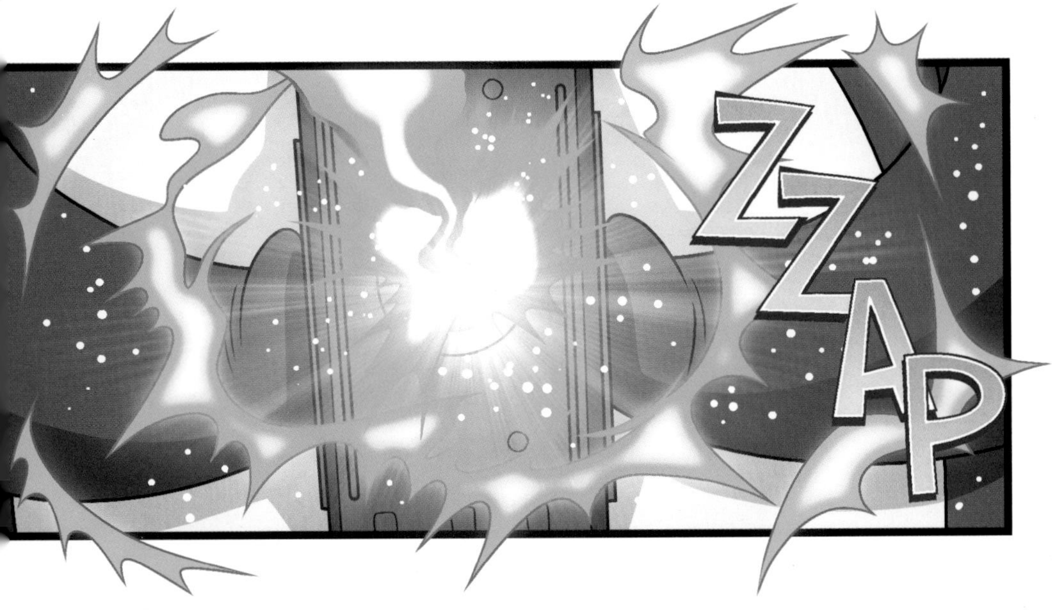
ZZZAP

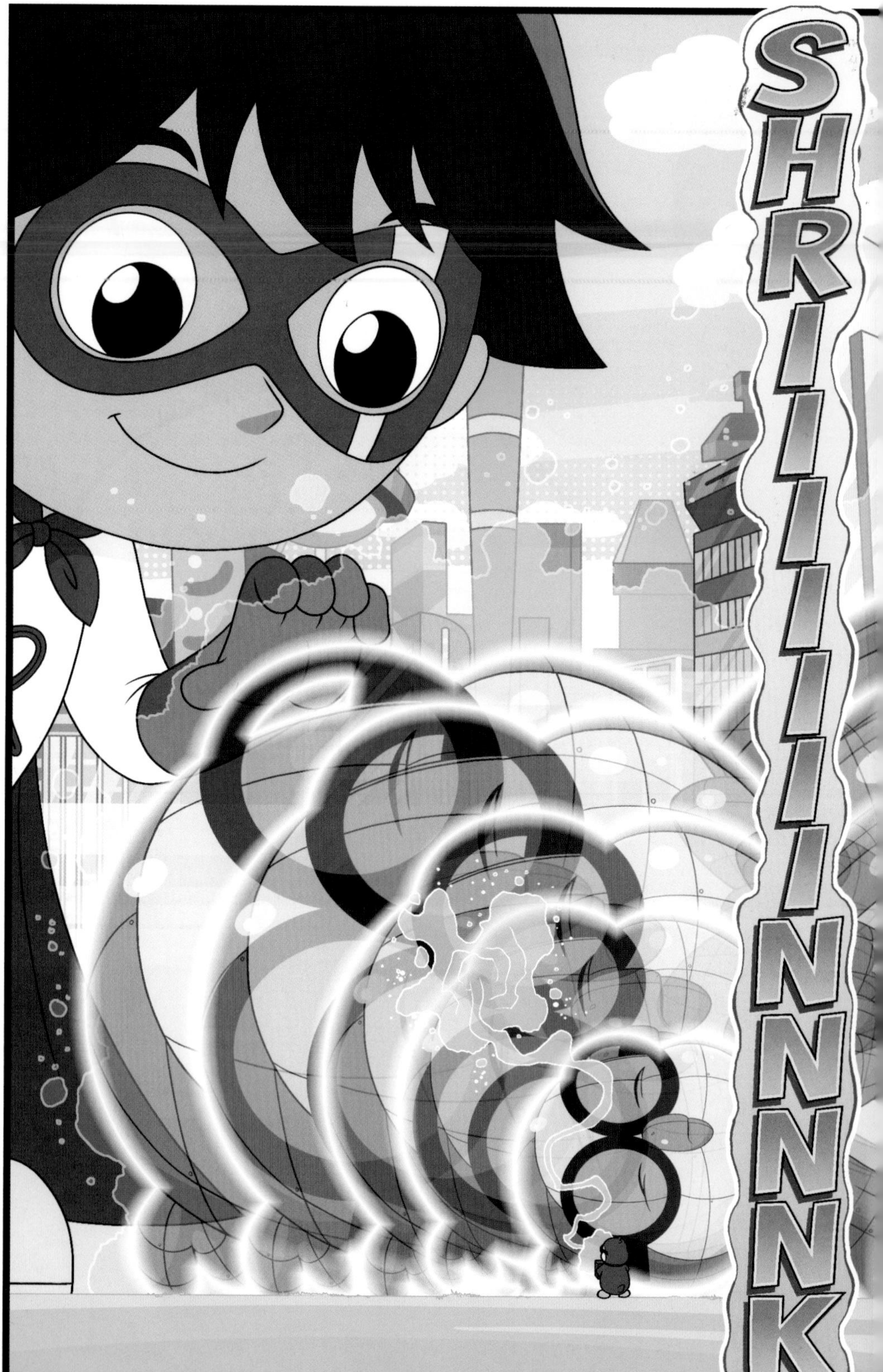
SHRIIIIINNNNK

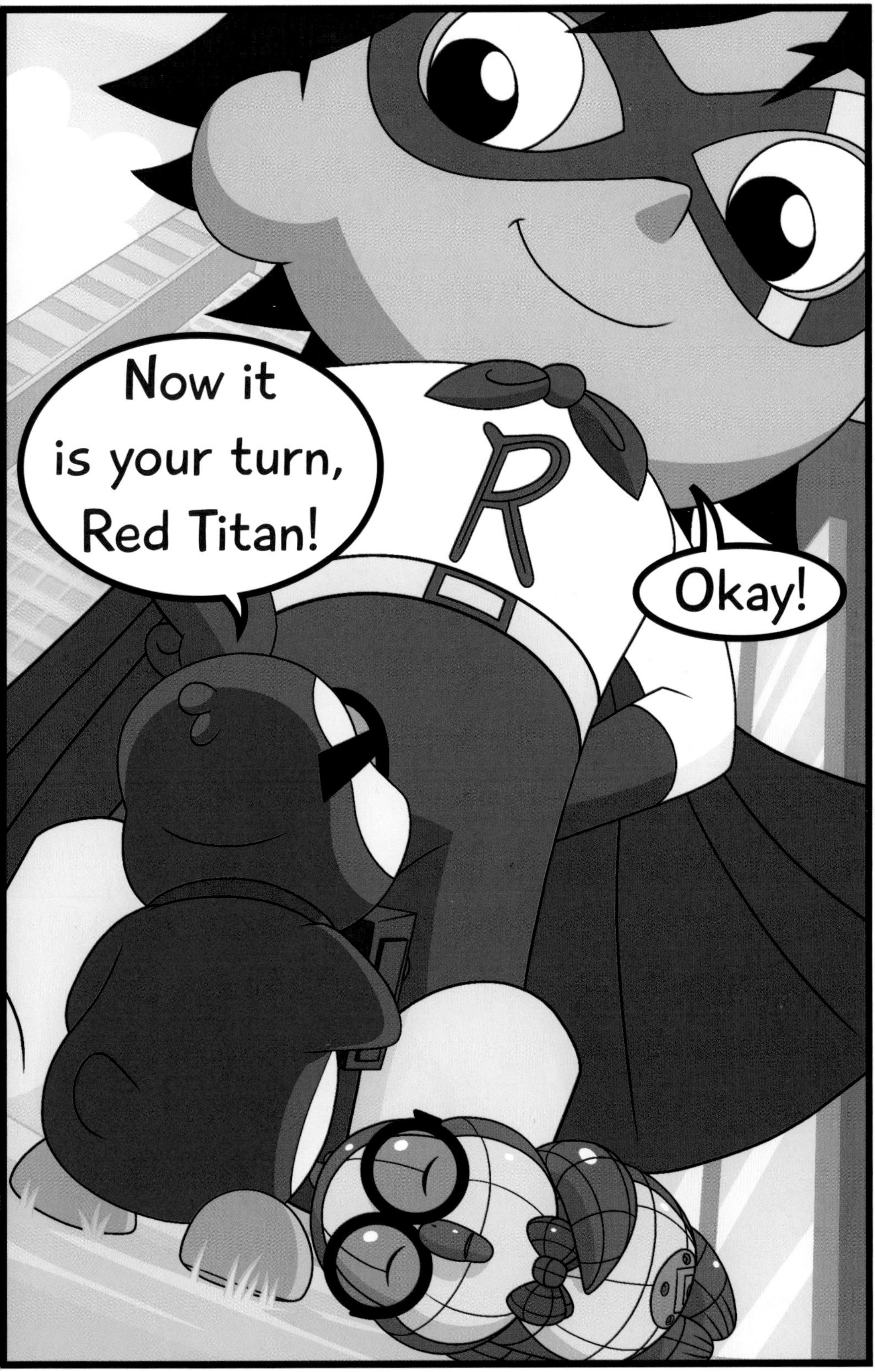
Now it is your turn, Red Titan!
Okay!

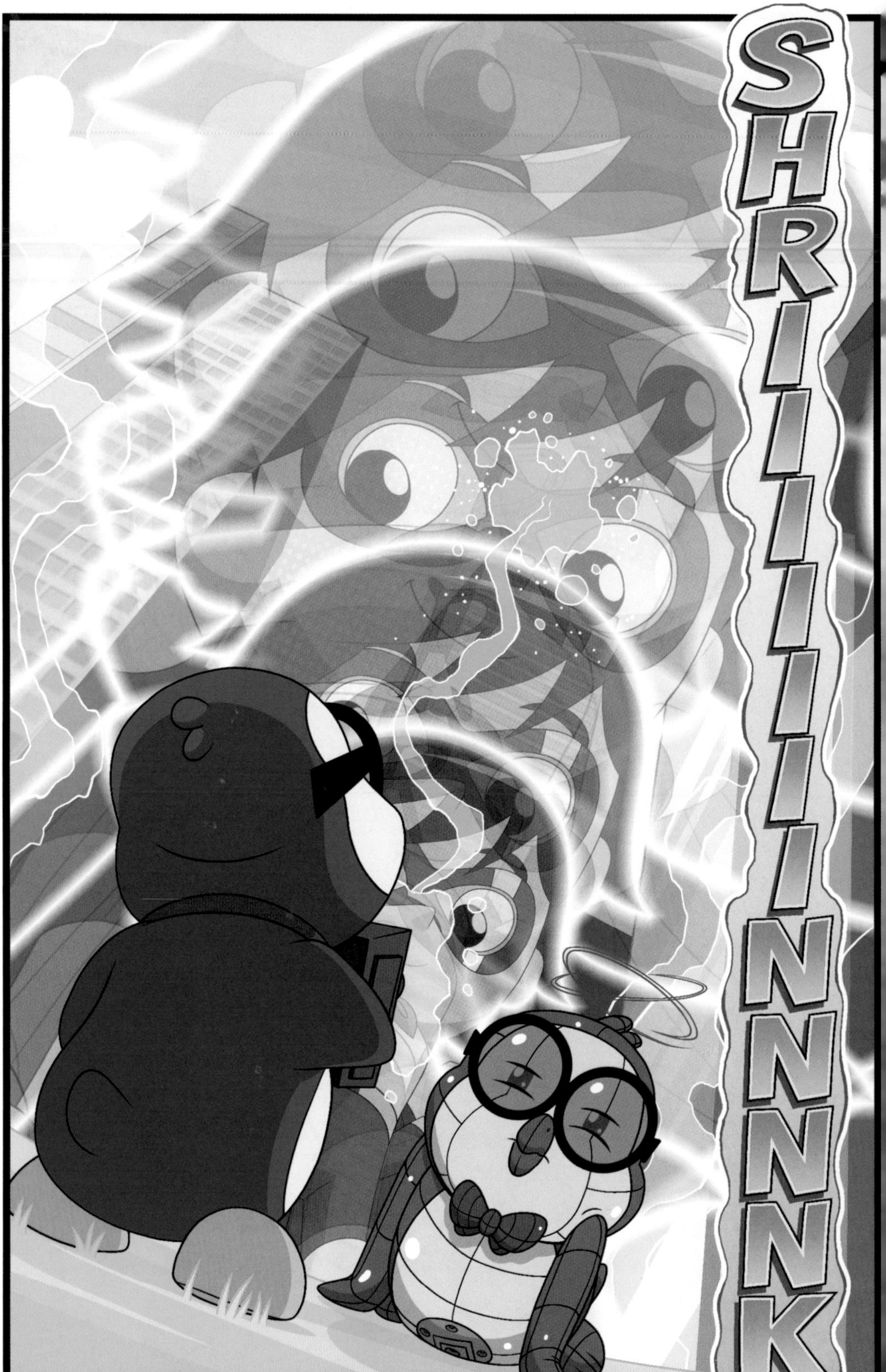
SHRIIIIIINNNK

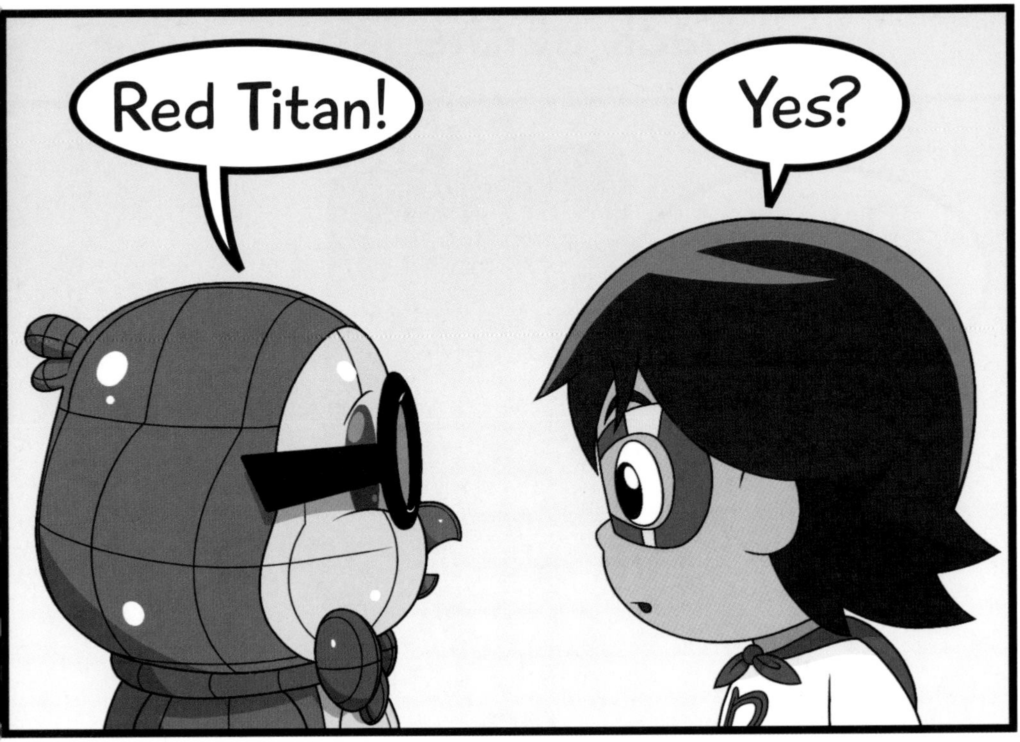
Red Titan!
Yes?

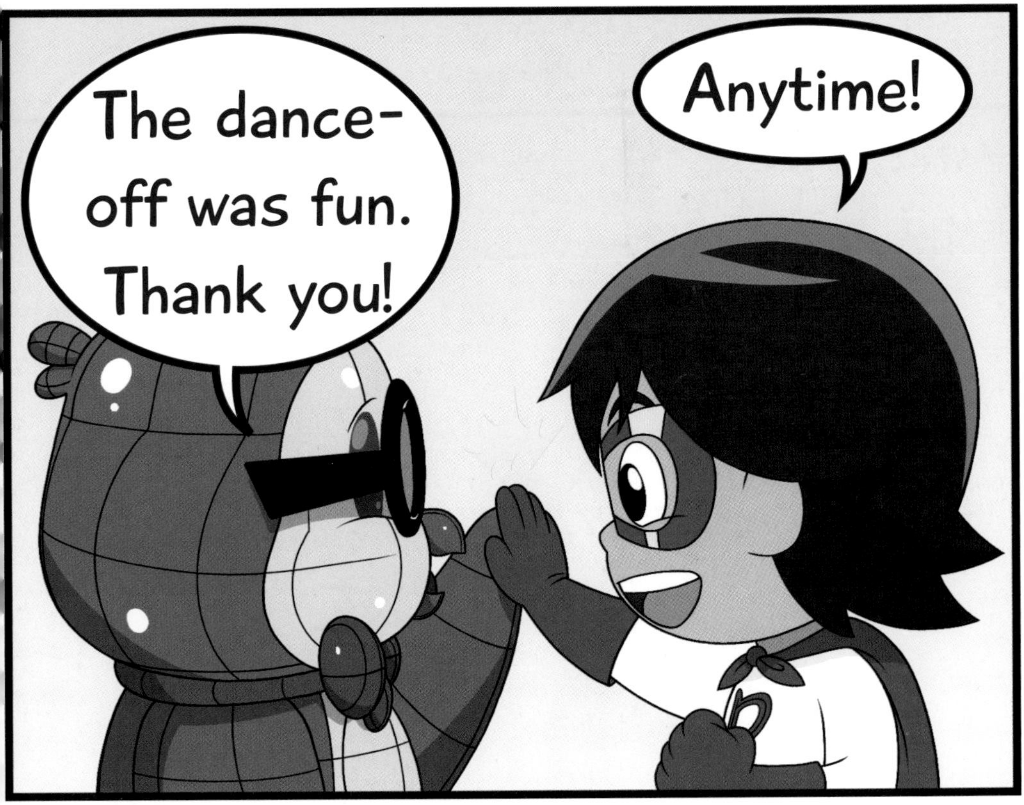
The dance-off was fun. Thank you!
Anytime!

Back at the lab...

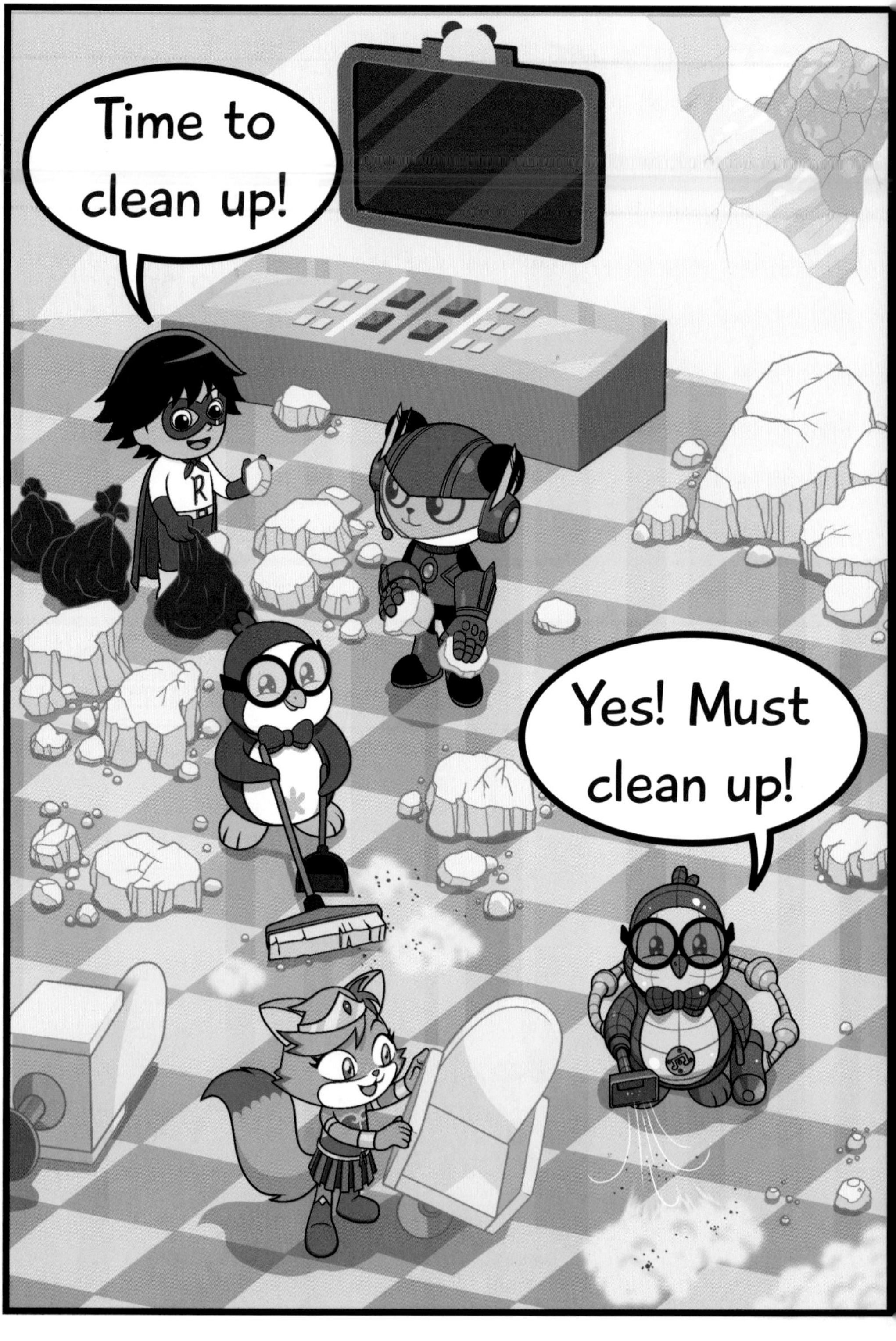
Time to clean up!
Yes! Must clean up!

Red Titan has saved the day!